Deadline for Justice

Evelyn Stonebridge

Contents

Chapter 1

3rd Moon

25th Phase

2018

6:45 am

It was a cold summer afternoon when my story began. Concluding my four-year studies in criminal investigation at the University of Kingstone, I was extended an invitation to undergo my first year on the field as an intern. My destination, Edinburgh, is the heart of the nearby country of Bogshire, where the company I have been assigned to work at is located. It is with that in mind that I have been riding for some time on the train, where my intention is to settle in on my private quarters and prepare myself for my first day starting tomorrow.

My name is Jennifer Hawkins. I am from Charlestown, Victoria and I am currently twenty-three years old. Surely, you might ask why, of all things, did I decide to go with this career? Ever since I can remember, I have always had a fascination with criminal investigations. Between my interest in the world of criminology and the zeal that Father once showed, you could say that it was inevitable I would end with this path I have chosen.

A few years ago, I had finished my general studies at the academy. And, as with every person of my age, it was my time to decide on my career choice in the last year. Knowing full well what I wanted to do with my life, I decided to let Mother know post haste. She was a bit apprehensive at first, as all parents usually are, but her blessings were given and I started to draw course towards my goal.

"Are you sure you are not interested in a career in writing?" asked my mother, recalling what I had told her before dinner.

"With how wild your imagination and creativity are, surely any press would publish the works you have done! Your full-fledged stories would do wonders for young children."

"Mother, I feel like you do not understand the difference between a hobby and a career," I said jokingly. "I do enjoy writing, but I lack the joy of making a career out of it. You know I always wanted to become an inspector like Father. His stories and adventures have always been of interest to me, and there has never been a more joyful time than when I stayed up late at night with him, sharing his tales with me. "

"I suppose so," she said hesitantly. "I just think you should focus on what you are naturally good at instead of deviating into uncharted territories. The real world is vastly different from a simple story, after all. Do pass me the dishes on the table, love, thank you."

Mother has always been protective of me. Being her only child would make sense why walls have been built around me since I can remember. And if you add the experience of loss with Father, well, it is a mix that any parent would grow anxious about the safety of their child, especially if the child in question is having the thought of going to a career filled with danger. I understand her, I truly do, but I had just turned seventeen, and I wanted to earn the sweat of my own brow doing the things that I have always dreamed of, not something I have no interest in making a profession out of.

Day after day I would ask her, and it was always met with a resounding no.

Finally, on a wistful night, I asked her again. She was growing frustrated as I kept bringing the same subject.

"When are you going to drop this? Why can you not see the bigger picture? Must I keep repeating myself?"

"But Mother please!" I begged.

"Do you want to be exposed to the danger? Have you not learned anything from what happened to your father? I know I have, and it has kept us both alive in one piece. Enough! if you bring this up again, I will most definitely confiscate all your belongings in regard to that dreaded workspace."

I was growing frustrated, ire. It is a feeling one goes through normally during that age, for it truly feels no one can understand how you are feeling. I was about to resign in dejection, but something came over me. It was like a something came towards my body, and spoke to me, pushing and imploring me to speak my mind, reminding me the desire I had to follow the same footsteps that Father went and that it was my goal to accomplish it no matter the cost. Mustering the words, an impulse came to me and I spoke.

"I... I understand how you feel. The thought of losing your only daughter after losing Father is heart shattering. It's a hole that can never be filled. But... I am not a child anymore and I want to become an investigator, like Father was. To experience what he experienced, feel what he felt, hoping that I might get close to him, even if it is little. I just want to try to do something he would be proud of. "

Barely being able to finish those words, I started to weep. I was seven years old when it happened, but even to this day it still feel like it was yesterday. These past years have been filled only with isolation, sadness and loneliness and it was just now that I was trying to expand my wings, even if it hurt. I was always closer to Father, you see, so the moment we heard that he had passed away, it felt like a part of my heart had been ripped apart.

Seeing my pitiful state, her face softened, pain enveloping her as she, too, understood how much this house feels empty without him. She longed for the embrace of her husband, and on days when she was alone in her room, she cried in silence, remembering how cold the bed had gotten, and how empty her world was the moment he was left. Giving a soft sigh, she gave me a comforting hug as I bawled. Picking up a tissue from the box on the counter, she cleaned my rosy cheeks.

"I know. I miss him too dear, I miss him too..."

In truth, Mother does not find anything wrong with the work field. With my inexperience in the field and danger I would be entering, it is no wonder she refuses to give me her blessings and would rather I study something that is safer. She might sometimes speak without consideration, but her intentions always mean well in the end.

In the city of Charlestown, she has always been well respected among her contemporaries. Her education is second to none, having acquired a doctorate in the medical field at only the age of twenty-one. Her form of speech is one to be commended, and her kindness towards children and elders has earned her the nickname 'Benevolence'. She is also not one to have an unpleasant appearance. Despite her age of forty-three, her beauty is still intact. Her back length amber hair, her natural womanly figure, and her defined face free from any wrinkles that often accompany people at her age have even men still falling for her to this day despite her age.

Even though she found herself to be a traditional woman, she was not one to be pushed around. From what I was told, she has always had a daring and resolved personality, something one would consider not expected from a woman of Victoria. And this further proves what I was told that she even accompanied Father and his friends on his private investigations not because she was only worried of him but because she enjoyed the thrill, she felt on their adventures together, a breath of fresh air from the monotony of her practice in the city and a horizon expanding upon the minute.

A few days pass and she gave it some thought, and after dinner she brought the topic in unexpectedly and said:

"You have his eyes, and his will for that matter," she smiled. "I was afraid that you would end up following his footsteps, but truthfully that was more denial than anything, for we both knew that one day this would happen. It is funny, you were always a shy and reserved child. Compared to the other children, you would prefer to be on your own. But whenever he spoke about his adventures, your mood would always change. It is frankly something I could never do with you whenever, despite trying my best."

A sense of nostalgia accompanied those words. Bittersweet feelings and melancholy were behind them as she reminisced about the days of the past.

"But you have grown, and who am I to stop you from making your own decisions? The best I can do now is give you my full unconditional support. Very well. If you want to become an investigator, then you have my blessing."

"Do you really mean it?!"

"I do," she answered with a smile. "I think it is very endearing that you wish to follow in his footsteps."

"Thank you so much!"

"However," she interjected sternly, "if you are being serious with this, then I expect you to pass with high grades. You might have this earnest goal, but I expect you to excel in all courses. So that means no nodding off or leaving things to the last minute. That also includes being responsible and having your appearance in an orderly fashion. No more of that introverted boorish attire. Your general online studies are done, and you are not to dress like that in any university, be it community college or the University of Victoria."

"But I like my boorish clothes! I feel so cozy whenever I have them on!"

"And you will not be wearing them. The least you can do is at least give some sort of respect for yourself and for the family."

//These terms...//

I was left annoyed at her conditions. But knowing full well that I should act more accordingly, I accepted it in the end.

"Okay, Okay," I sighed, "if it will let me go study then fine."

"Very good then. Now! Help me clean these dishes, Jennifer. The sooner we finish here, the sooner we can start searching for applicable universities that teach this. Hm? What are you standing there for? Come, come, before I change my mind! "

After a few hours, I finally decided to send my admission papers to the University of Victoria. Managing to achieve a response and passing the qualifier exam, I commenced my studies on the University of Victoria on Queensville.

After diligently studying for four years in this painstaking course, I managed to pass all my evaluations and graduate without a problem. A certain organization by the name of the Collective Detective Agency suddenly sent the letter, inviting me to work with them on my intern. Never hearing from them, I decided to look up the organization, to which proved to be so little information, that my suspicious were aroused, thinking this could have possibly been a prank from my classmates. To my surprise, however, came my Mother, telling me to accept the invitation. She understood why I was being cautious, but she pushed me to accept for, she was confidant that they would help my career grow. After giving it some thought, I accepted and immediately contacted them to coordinate when should I start.

And here we are today. With a set of clothes Mother had picked up for me, I decided to give it a go. An ivory trench coat, a striped dress shirt, a simple aqua tie to and my favorite brown boots. In the end, after packing my belongings and getting ready for the journey I am to embark, we both headed towards the nearby train station. Before saying my goodbyes, Mother had remembered something she had left in the car and came about in quick fashion. She returned and brought Father's old newsie cap. I was left in shock, for I had thought that it had been lost from his last adventure. Judging by the look she gave me, I knew she wanted me to take it and where it as I began my career.

"He would have wanted for you to have it," she smiled as she said that. "Just think of it as your good luck charm, so you can feel at peace whenever you feel nervous."

"Thank you, Mother." I hugged her with all my heart.

"I promise I will be a daughter you both will be proud of. I will miss you and I will call you the moment I arrive. Love you forevermore."

"Love you forevermore, dear."

With the train arriving on time, I get onboard to wave Mother goodbye, noticing small tears falling from her cheeks. With the train announcer signaling to commence the trip, it slowly but surely starts to ramp up speed, what seemed mere moments turning into distant time. With the train on time, we march towards my destination, the country without limits, Bogshire. In no less than five hours, I arrive timely without a problem to share about. Exiting the station, I was then introduced to the bustling, diverse crowds I have heard so much about. Be it because of poverty, social or political reasons, people from various countries come together here to have a chance at a new life, having finally the chance to start from the beginning and controlling their own future from scratch. With so much movement at this hour of the day, it became apparent that it would be wise to take action and hail a cab, for, I feared that if I was to stay longer at the entrance, I'd be entranced to explore and forget what I was supposed to do. Calling a cabbie to my directions, we head eastbound to where the Collective Detective Agency had marked where my private quarters was located. Retrieving the key that they so kindly left me, I pick it up from inside the mailbox, taking my time to settle in completely after a long day.

With an hour, I finally leave out an exhausting sigh, catching my breath after a long day.

"I have to admit," I spoke to myself, "while I am not one to feel confident with my abilities, I must say everything worked out in top conditions. In only six hours, no less!"

"Kitchen, check."

"Bedroom filled with stuffed animals, check."

"Coping corner with snacks and tissues, triple check!"

"And finally, Carlos, my trusty cactus friend, neatly set on the night table in case I need to use it as a weapon for intruders!" I chuckled with heart.

I am not one to possess much zeal, but I will admit that I felt much accomplished after a long day. Between finally living alone, moving into my apartment, and almost finishing the course after six years of brutal studying, I did feel proud that I did this all on my own. It truly felt like I was finally taking my first steps into adulthood.Taking in everything that has transpired, hunger suddenly came upon my mind. Without much delay, I ordered some takeout from the nearby food market, concluding the day with something to eat, a bath and a good night's rest.

Chapter 2

3rd Moon
26th Phase
2018
8:21 am

It was a brilliant day. As the morning star had settled, its piercing rays of light cut through the windowsill, caressing me to to wake up and begin my first day. After a breakfast I had neatly prepared with some coffee, I collected my newsie cap and messenger bag, clicking the front door open as the light covered my face in all its glory. Strolling around the Hillside block -where my lodgings are situated- I crossed the street towards Oxford Square, where I was to rendezvous with a fellow agent of the Agency. Considering that I had arrived earlier than expected, I decided to sit on the nearby bench, where the song of birds and the playing of children was rather resounding but charming, nonetheless. A few minutes pass and suddenly my attention shifts towards an oddly dressed girl in blue approaching me without apprehension.

She was a woman of average build with a small stature. Her hair was as blue as the azure skies and her hair was as curvy as the roaring waves, shoulder length to be precise. Even if her eyes were kept by the glasses she wore, her eyes were as pure and beautiful as sapphire. Her attire was simple, but comfortable. A scientific gown blended with what seemed to be a cute dress with frills underneath it. She wore stockings and what seemed to be a pair of moccasins. She might have looked to be past her teenage years.

"Hey!" she called, "Might you perhaps be Ms. Hawkins?"

"Er, and who is asking exactly?"

"Wellll, I may or not may not be a member of the CDA. However, before I say anything, I have to find out if you're the one we're expecting to meet. Lots of people have been impersonating agents in these past months and committing crimes in our names with the purpose of giving us a bad reputation throughout the districts."

"Oh! I was unaware that such crimes were taking place in Bogshire."

"Right? Not only is it bad business, but it's also annoying for everyone. Well, fortunately, I brought myself a little doohickey that'll help set matters straight."

Picking her backpack, she started perusing the tools and equipment she had collected from the Agency. I must confess that I was becoming rather anxious at the distraction, for it was getting a tad late from the appointed time included in the instructions.

"I understand why you are taking the necessary precautions but should not just showing you my papers be sufficient for-"

"Ah-ha!" the odd woman exclaimed, "Say hello to the Identity! With this baby, I can tell anyone from anything from just the look on their face!"

"Really now!"

I have always had an interest in modern day technology. Science magazines were somewhat of a pass time for me growing up, and I more often than not enjoyed doing school projects with my classmates. So you can see that learning that such devices were being made by the organization I was to work with piqued my interest, making me forget that I was running against the clock.

"Okay, now hold still and make sure to close your eyes. Thank you! If you don't, then the light of it might leave you blind."

"Blind?!"

"Relax, that's like, what, a twenty percent chance? It'll be fine!"

//Twenty percent chance? This is absurd, my first day at work and I'm already exposing myself to a chance of losing my sight. Not much I can do, I suppose. Might as well just get it over it.//

As soon as I closed my eyes, the stranger pressed a button, and the device started working. Lights started to dance in front of my eyelids and the constant noises it was making showed that it was doing its intended purpose. If I am to be honest, I was a feeling a bit nervous and impatient. But if achieving my dreams required to pass this examination, then so be it. Or that's what I initially thought. As soon as I thought those words, all I heard was nonsensible garble. Confused, I slowly opened my eyes to only be greeted by my acquaintance laughing her lungs out, to which -if I might add- provoked the attention of everyone near us. Astonished, I was left seeking an answer.

"Ha-ha-ha! Wow! I can't believe you actually felled for that! No one usually falls for this, but you took the bait like a champ!" she said in between her laughter.

I was growing furious at this childish rubbish. Here I was, nervous on my first day, waiting anxiously to start my journey, and here I am wasting time on her shenanigans.

"I'm sorry! I'm sorry, ha-ha! But knowing that I was left in charge of bringing the newbie to the building, I just had to prank you on your first day! I couldn't just pass it up!"

She gave a mischievous smile.

"Come now! I am running late to meet with the Director, and you are here performing these charlatan routines!" I cried in frustration.

"Ha-ha, I know, I know, and I'm sorry for that. I'm done now though, so no more pranks from my end! Promise!"

"Ugh. So where is the Agency exactly?"

"Oh, it's not too far off from here. It's only a twenty minute drive, and the car is waiting for us, so we should be fine. Now! I think some introductions are in order."

With a twirl and a jump, the impish girl struck a pose, introducing herself.

"My name is Pelagic Okeanos. Pleasure to meet you!"

I will admit, that was probably the most bizarre form of introduction I have ever witnessed. I always thought the agents of the CDA were to be more serious and professional. But upon going through such an ordeal and now this, I was left concerned with what I was to expect in working with this Agency.

"In any case," she interjected, "the company car is waiting over there, so let's get a move on and not make Raoul wait for us any longer."

"Company car?"

"Yup! With how big Bogshire is, we have a personal transportation service managed by Raoul. There wasn't any traffic when we got here, so I think that we should be there in fifteen minutes. Here, let me get you the door."

"Oh, um, thank you."

The elder gentleman in question was a rather old bush browed individual whose age and wrinkles seem to suggest a man of experience. His most defining features, however, was the monocle he possessed on his left eye and the extravagant moustache that dressed his face. With a dignified air to him, in part to his black blazer and white dress shirt, I could not help but stare in awe.

"Good morning mistress Hawkins." he greeted warmly.

"You know who I am?"

"But of course. What kind of driver would I be if I did not know who my clients are? I was told by the Director that I was to pick you up with Okeanos here, although it seems that it has become rather late compared to what it was initially stipulated. Mistress Okeanos, might the reason be because of you?"

"What?? Nah, she just got kinda lost is all!"

//Um, no?//

Shaking his head in dissapointment, he shares a sigh, clearly displaying that this is not the first time that this has happened. "I apologize on behalf of everyone if she has been trouble. Unfortunately, whenever she gets in one of her moods, she promises a challenging experience for everyone, and not the enjoyable kind. I hope, however, that this does not share a negative image of the Agency. Unless I knew beforehand, I would have stopped her sooner."

"It sounds like you speak of experience."

"You have no idea."

"Eh?! Raoul, what's that supposed to mean?!" she cried, surprised.

"Ha-ha, pardon me. Well, the trip is a rather short one, so until we get there, feel free to entertain yourself with mistress Okeanos. She can be quite a handful, but she is a very kind child nonetheless."

"Raoul, can you please stooop."

Laughing with joy, he closes the window connecting the passenger and driver.

"Ugh, he's always treating me like a kid. Anyway, if it's alright with you, I would like to get to know you more than we ride. We have some refreshments here as well, so please help yourself."

"Oh, thank you."

Despite the first impressions of a devilish imp, she had possessed courtesy at least to treat well others, which in return helped make the drive more enjoyable.

We made some small talk regarding our hobbies. Surprisingly, those fifteen minutes were what we needed to break the ice. From what I have gathered, she enjoys partaking in the arts, specifically watercolor. She showed me a sketch she had photographed from her telephone and what I saw left me verily impressed. A beautiful, lush forest was the scenery it enveloped as the fawn was bathed in security by her mother and the surrounding trees that shared it comfort. With the flora surrounding the pair, filled with primroses and foxgloves, you could feel the serenity the picture brought to the viewer. It was a hugely impressive work of art, especially if you consider that she ha no academic background. What her role in the Collective Detective Agency is however played on my mind as she continued to talk with me.

Finally, after some time, a huge building became visible, with a tall sign displaying the words 'The Collective Detective Agency'.

It was a structured, well-established building. It presented a very modern design that resonated with what I have seen so far from this country. It possessed a few details like the window panels and accents that reminded me of the architecture you are accustomed to see in my country, Victoria, but with a few personal design choices that made it entirely unique. On the drop off point was an array of flowers and statues, each possibly having their own sort of history. Upon entering the lobby, Raoul parks the car so that we could enter the building.

"Fascinating," I muttered, impressed.

We exited the vehicle and proceeded to enter the lobby, where a lone fountain was standing in the center. It was a quiet room and the only noises we could hear was the sound what I presume to believe coming from the earphones of the receptionist in front.

"Well! That's as far as tour guide Okeanos will take you!" interjected Ms. Okeanos.

"You're not coming?"

"Sorry, I can't. The Chief from Research and Development has been trying to contact me since we picked you up so I'm guessing something important came up at the lab."

"Oh, I hope you have not gotten to any trouble because of me."

"Hm? Oh look at you, you're worried about me! And here I thought you hated me!"

//This woman...//

"He-he, oh don't worry about that. I'll be fine. And anyway, if I did get in trouble, then it was because of me. I wanted to welcome you into our little agency and, -besides doing my little prank, get to know you a bit. I can see that you're a very nice person. A little quiet considering your job requires you to talk and deal with the public almost half the time, but a very responsible person, nonetheless. From what I can see, though, I think you'll fit in on the Investigation Division quite nicely."

"Thank you for the kind words. In return, I will make sure to take into consideration your input."

Sharing an honest smile, I could not help but smile back enjoying our little time together.

"You should go check in with Hypno. He's the one who handles paperwork, who goes in and out, that sort of stuff. He doesn't look like a very appealing guy, but he can be very sweet once you get to know him. He'll give you the ID for clearance on all our facilities, the map, all that sort of stuff. Oh right! We should exchange contacts so we can message each other in case you need assistance or just want to talk."

"O-oh, um, sure yeah."

Getting our phones together, we linked our accounts and became friends on the messaging service.

"Done! We're iBuddies now! Like I said, if you ever need help, please give me a call. I'll do my best to answer you as soon as possible."

Knowing that she seemed genuine with those words, I could not help but appreciate the gesture. Despite her devilish personality, she ended being an exceedingly kind and serviceable girl.

"Well, I'll be seeing you. Stay safe and I hope everything goes well on your first day!"

With a wave to her goodbye, she proceeded to descend onto a set of stairs next to a pair of elevators, possibly towards the Research and Development division. Although I am intrigued by what such division entails, I refrained my curiosity, for the meeting proved to be of utmost importance and would prefer to not delay anymore that I have already done.

After having a moment to collect my thoughts, I took a deep breath and went onward to meet the receptionist. He seemed to be focused on a task at the computer. His ability to not notice was rather obvious, considering he had his earphones plugged in since I got here. Calling for his attention proved to be fruitless, for no hand signs or high voice could do enough to make him shift his glance.

Losing patience, I take a deep breath to calm myself down. It was then that I noticed a small but cute bell next to the computer. Considering my options, I opted to ring for it, again, again and again until he finally looked up, -although in annoyance, and noticed my presence.

"Yes?" he said, irritated.

"Good morning, my name is Jennifer Hawkins, and I was invited to work here as an intern. I was hoping to obtain the identification for the facilities as well as all other information addressed to me. I would appreciate it if you could help me-"

"Is that so?" he replied in a dismissive tone as he continued to work.

//Did he seriously go back to work? This is becoming tiresome. What kind of service is this? It is like he is doing it on purpose! Ugh, maybe if I keep ringing the bell, he might...//

I focused my gaze with the intent of provoking his attention as I continued to ring the bell. As childish as this tactic was, I simply did not care. With his face contorting in anger, I ring one more time, slamming the desk in exasperation.

"Can you stop the damn ringing!?" he sneered. "If you have eyes, you can clearly see I'm in the middle of work. Hello? Clearly something you might not know what is considering you've got nothing else to do than MAKE NOISE. If I had the time to reply to your 'pressing inquiries' I would have done by now, now wouldn't I? Now buzz off, I ain't got the time for tourists, Princess."

//Princess?!//

His rude behavior was even worse than I imagined. He was a young man, no older than Ms. Okeanos. He was not particularly attractive, but he was also not necessarily that repulsive... not that I care anyway. He had a sharp face and was clean shaved, lacking in any cuts or impurities. His hair was wild but kept, no longer than ear length, fused with a mix of a natural chestnut brown with a highlight of reddish wine on his bangs. He was of average height, somewhat taller than Ms. Okeanos, but not as tall as me. He sported a pretty comfortable fashion, having only a sweatshirt, some hanging belts and brown khakis, a distinct clip on earring on his left ear and a pair of bracelets on his right hand.

"I understand," I replied with a frustrated smile, "but I believe there is no need for me to receive an attitude when I just want you to offer me the identification that has been given to you. It is obvious that you have it since the Agency was expecting my arrival. Can you not just check if you have it in one of your drawers, please?"

"What kind of 'I can't' do you not get? Like I said, I'm in the middle of something. I don't care who you are or where you're from, but if you need something, go call our phone lines. Otherwise, buzz off."

I will admit, I have never been one to be patient with people and surely there is fault in me for it. But he was getting on my nerves, and I was about to give him a piece of my mind until someone approached us.

"Oi Hypno, are you pickin' up fights again? There's no need for that. After all, what would happen if the higher ups knew you scared off the rook with that sour attitude of yours?"

She was a tall, tanned woman whose chestnut hair resembled a semblance of an autumn leaf. She sported a pseudo athletic winter outfit, covering herself with a broken down brown fur hoodie that covered her right side, whatever remaining visible being covered by a black compressed shirt and some mid length black leggings. She had a beautiful long braid that covered her freckled right-side cheek and whatever remained, resting on her left shoulder.

"Tch, Ciarda," he responded with disdain, "It ain't my fault. You know how rush hour is on this day of the week. I'm on a deadline now and things like these take priorities, especially when the one who ordered me to do this are those same higher ups you just mentioned. If you're so worried about her, why don't you help her around? Besides, Aether ain't here, so it's not she's gonna get anything done."

//The Director is not here? //

"Ha-ha, got me there! However, considering that the entire Agency was expecting for the rook to appear, this should have been the highest priority of our lovely receptionist as well. Besides, have you forgotten who is in charge today? The same guy who constantly nags you to death, rats you out to the Director and more often than not ends up fighting you. What would happen if, oh I don't know, told him that you didn't attend the rook?"

"You're bluffing. You wouldn't dare."

"Try me."

There was a silence for a few seconds. What seemed like a western showdown ended in less than two minutes. As the triumphant woman smiles confidently, the challengers attitude dissolves into a submissive sigh filled with nothing but groans.

"Pain in the rear," he muttered between his teeth. "Ugh, fine, whatever..."

What seemed to be a rebellious teen turned into a whimpering dog at the mercy of the woman in plaids.

"Great! That's our lovely receptionist!" She cried.

"Go to hell."

Although I lacked the context of the threat, I nonetheless appreciated the gesture shared by the stranger.

"I appreciate your assistance Ms.?"

"Ciarda, name's Ciarda," she answered with a prideful smile.

"Right, thank you Ms. Ciarda."

"It's no problem at all but um, do try to lose the Ms. lass. There's no reason to have formalities, well, at least around these parts, " she said smiling. "Ah, I do apologize for this eejits attitude, though."

"Eejit?"

"Eejit, it's what in Bogshire we call a special kind of idiot."

"Ah."

"Yeah, don't worry about him. He might act like that, but he's not a bad guy by any means, just a doofus for the most part when it comes to talking to people. In any case, if you feel grateful, how about you pop one up for me at the pub after you're done with your onboarding, eh?"

"Excuse me?"

"Nyahaha!"

//Yeah, respectful was not the right choice of word, more like captivated by the reward.//

"What a laugh. Having said all that, welcome to the Collective Detective Agency. We're a relatively new organization that just started working seventeen years ago. Our center is here at the heart of Bogshire, Edinburgh. We have a few offices across the country, but this here is home. We hope to expand and work internationally with the neighboring countries and their respective Governmental Police Offices. Right now, though, we're staying local, solving crimes in the country and staying hard in the R and D division trying to develop new tools and devices to help our investigations reach conclusions easier and faster. Seeing that criminals are always on the up and up, it's our job to help the local Government Police Force achieve results that are to be proud of, keeping our fellows protected and safe. Ah, it seems Hypno is done with the process. See was that so hard? In any case, have at it, lass."

After this whole charade ended, I was finally able to receive my identification, giving me clearance towards the main facilities such as the Research and Development Floor, the

Directors Office, Medical Room and my own personal office space.

"Heh, oh, right," she smiled as she remembered something, "I'm sure ol' Pelly forgot to mention this, but that identification is a placeholder. You're bound to get the real deal once you pass your preliminary test."

"I beg your pardon?"

"What, have you never heard of onboard tests? And here I thought you were all gung-ho and ready."

"I know what that is!" I exclaimed. "What I meant was that I was not made aware of any trials that I had to pass. I was told that the documents and papers would et me begin my internship, but not in that particular detail."

"Ah, well, the reason is that normally students like yourself tend to shy away from the challenge, so I guess they omitted that detail. They don't like the idea of solving a case from the get-go. That or working directly with a special someone, heh."

"Solve a case?!"

At the sudden news, I was beginning to feel a chill down my spine. Not because it was a challenge, but because I was to solve a case on my first day. I had considered my abilities, so the thought of solving a case never crossed my mind. Reading the room, Hypno let out an exasperated sigh and made a slightly comforting remark.

"Look, just relax he sighed. I can understand why you feel a bit nervous. Lord knows when I started working in this joint, I was left dumbfounded by the sound of that nonsense. However, that's how things work around here. We're not your typical black and white cop department, so we do things a little out of the norm. But know that out of all the people that we considered working with us, you were the one selected."

"If you can show the same attitude you showed me, you'll be fine."

"Yeah, you'll be fine! If Hypno here got a job, then I'm pretty sure a dandy lass like you will do great today!"

"You know you can be a real pain sometimes," he responded appaled.

Even though I had just met them and my first impression of them was not as favorable as I had hoped, they did show that they were not all bad people. Ciarda seemed like a loose cannon, but she had a big sister air to her. And Hypno is... a weird one. I do not really know exactly how he is like, but I can see he has a heart beneath those harsh words.

"I see. Thank you for the kind words." I said sheepishly.

"Of course!"

"Hmph."

"Well! Now, with that settled, I should go. Snowy and I have an operation on the Southwest Drive canal. Kaguya reported that some drug activities will be taking place tonight, so I have to prepare as much as I can with her. Now that you have the map, lass, you should check it when you get the chance. But before anything, you should head to the Director's Office and meet with the man in charge. It's on the 3rd floor of the 12th suite. Like Hypno said, the Director isn't here at the moment so you will be meeting with Lucio."

"Lucio?" I asked.

"Yep! He's the Ace of the Investigation Division and the man left in charge for today. He's a wee bit aloof, but deep down he has a golden heart. He can act a bit distant sometimes, but it's usually whenever he's thinking of stuff, usually work related. So, if you see him in his thoughts, do wait for a wee bit. I'm sure if you do, he'll be more receptive towards you. In any case, I gotta get a move on and not keep Snowy waiting. Good luck!"

She waved and disappeared into a door on the right-side of the building. As she left, Hypno got back into his working position and responded as he continues to work.

"You know the way, so go ahead. I paged Allegro earlier and left him a message, though I think that airhead might have not noticed it. Good luck."

Biding my farewells, I decided to make my way as instructed by Ciarda. Fighting the butterflies in my stomach, I push on, trying to maintain my calm composure as I ascend to meet with the person who will be overseeing me today.

Chapter 3

3rd Moon

26th Phase

2018

9:45 am

Upon reaching the second floor, I was finally presented with the mahogany door where I was to meet with the man in charge for today. Without further delay, I slowly pushed the door open, creaking, as the interior of the room became visible to me, welcoming me inside to enjoy the warm and comfortable atmosphere it brought upon itself. In its delightful presentation accompanied however a mysterious lone figure, sitting behind the desk, the sunlight penetrating throughout the glass panes that gave him the long shadow that loomed over the entire room. He appeared to be in the middle of some deep thought, not paying mind to his surroundings as I stood at the entrance. No, I believe the correct term should be brooding, for his face was as serious as it could have been, and his lips quivered rapidly.

With his arms crossed and his head stooping towards the desk, the only sound that could be heard was the crackling of the fireplace and the ticking of the grandfather clock. Remembering the words Ciarda shared with me, I settled myself on a chair and waited near the fireplace until he had was done. Perhaps it was a case he had been working on? Or maybe he was performing mental exercise as he waited for me? Whichever the case may be, I waited patiently until he was done.

It was not until three minutes passed when he finally opened his eyes, when he became aware of my presence. And with a quick glimpse, he already knew who I was.

"Ah," he finally said, "so you're the fresh blood we were expecting. I apologize on behalf of the Director for not appearing for today's meeting. He has been away for some time, for some urgent matters had arisen, and he had to attend it as quickly as possible."

"So I heard. Which is why I was told that you would be attending me for these few days."

"Hm, so you've been informed. Good, then this speeds up things considerably."

He was a man of average stature, being roughly the same height as me. He had a somewhat wide chest, but not wide enough to be overbearing. His hair was mid length, silky and had a tone of caramel. His beautiful eyes were as brilliant as the color of the sun, and his naturally handsome face was further accentuated by the beauty mark he had on his left cheek. His dress code showed a simple but comfortable attire. A lavender turtleneck sweater, some black pants and some brown boots, with his hand accessorized by a small silver ring.

"Er Ms. Hawkins? You seem to have gone daydreaming for a second there. I hope that you aren't wont to do this sort of thing when you start working with us. In any case, you appear to be late."

"I apologize. I was dragged a bit because certain events transpired on my way towards here."

"Was it Okeanos who brought you here?"

"Yes, why?"

"Then never mind," he shook his head.

"Huh?"

"I was told that someone was assigned by the Director to pick you up, but I was not aware that it would her. If there was any other reason, then there would have been issues. But seeing Okeanos was your escort, it would be fair to conclude that you got dragged into her nonsense."

"You could say that," I said sheepishly.

He gave a sigh.

"In any case, it's a pleasure to meet you, Miss Jennifer Hawkins. Ah, but my manners. My name is Lucio Allegro, and I will be your superior until you feel familiar working with us. Until you get used to the agency, feel free to let me know if you need help with anything."

"Of course, thank you!"

"Hm, I knew that we were getting a rookie with promising talent, but I was left astonished when it turned to be the daughter of 'Golden Sight'".

"'Golden Sight'? Wait, might you be talking about Father?"

"Naturally, that was the nickname of John Hawkins, after all."

I was caught in shock at what he had ascertained. For starters, I did not expect someone so young to know about my Father, and even less know I was his daughter. I have not exactly talked about him nor it would someone who people might now across country, so how in the devil did he know about all that?

"Excuse me, but how exactly did you know about my Father? And for that manner, know I was his daughter?"

"Hm? Well, it's obvious, is it not?" he replied confidently.

"That newsie, in particular, clearly shows a state of use. The cotton, for starters, is absolutely stretched out and compared to the size of your head, it encompasses a much larger space, meaning it had to originate from someone else, more specifically a man. Assuming it's a man, we can safely say it's your father, for parents tend to leave items to their next of kin as a parting gift, good luck charm, or even to remember them by. And that person, no doubt, was John Hawkins' ex investigator from the governmental police department of Victoria, Georgetown. Between his rather iconic newsie cap when he was a young lad and because you pertain his unique golden eyes -something not that common- it was safe to jump to this conclusion."

I was impressed by how he got all that information just by simply looking at my eyes and hat. To a certain extent, I would say he was reading more than he was allowed. But, I would lie if I did not admit I was verily impressed by his keen observations.

"That and I read your onboarding papers."

"Ah."

//Nevermind...//

Still, even if he did read my background, it is still rather intriguing how he could mention all these little details just by just simply looking, especially someone who is younger than me.

"Well, you have done your homework. Regardless, I do not see what that has to do with my onboarding right now."

"Fair point. I just found it interesting why the daughter of 'Golden Sight' was selected above everyone else. Well, no matter." he paused as he got up from his chair.

"You have come far and wide no doubt," he spoke as he drank what seemed to be a drink he had prepared.

"However, as I'm sure you've been told, we do things around here differently."

//Here we go...//

"We believe that results can be achieved from experience. So instead of filling the boring papers today, you're going to be assisting me in solving a murder case."

He carried himself, picking his belongings as he prepared himself for the venture.

"W-with all due respect, sir, I am not sure I qualify enough to start on my first day working on a case with you. I had just arrived, and I have had no particular training beforehand."

"Come now, everyone starts from somewhere. No one is born with experience. It's all about the practice. So the sooner you start, the sooner you'll master the craft."

"And I understand that, sir, but I just believe this is too much for it being my first day. I am not sure I feel like I can do this at all."

He raised a questioning eyebrow.

"What were you expecting? To hold your hand and go take you to some fish and chips?"

//Can you be considerate for a bit here? Why do you have to be so mean?//

"If you are going to be working with us, you must be accustomed to how we do things around here. We're constantly overwhelmed by the number of cases we receive, and we need all the help we can afford. We might have been functioning for more than six years, but we're still relatively small when it comes to personnel and recognition. If you feel like this is too much for you, feel free to leave and go back to Victoria. We have no need for people who can't even put in the work when the situation calls for it."

//Ugh...//

Even though his words were as harsh as the asphalt on the roads, I still felt that there was some truth in them. I will admit that I was overwhelmed by all the characters I had just started meeting, but meeting Mr. Allegro takes it all. There was a sense of authority whenever he was present, and an intimidating nature I was not used to, nor I wanted to get used to. I wanted to respond, but I knew that would be in vain, for my nerves were getting ahold of me and I could not find the right words to express. However, as I touched Father's soft hat, I remembered the words he told me from long ago:

//"Always remember to remain calm. If you are calm, everything will be clear, and you will surely overcome any obstacle that comes your way. Remember this, and you will in turn begin to progress in whatever story life takes you."//

Remembering those recollected words, I drew a deep breath, collected myself and gave resounding response:

"Very well, if this is the way how things work here, then I will adjust myself and follow how the Agency works."

I was a bit shaken, if I am to admit, but my resolute response was more than enough to stabilize my mind. Satisfied, he softened his gaze a little and nodded in agreement.

"Good, then we're off," he said with approval in his voice, "Hypno has called up the company cab and it should be arriving no less than five minutes. Ah, speak of the devil it appears its already waiting for us. Come along miss Hawkins for this will be a drive. Our stop will be on Williams Road in Brixton County. We are to meet with the officers, so let us not delay any longer."

Returning to the lobby, we noticed our chauffer waiting for us outside. With Mr. Allegro telling her the directions, we left towards the House of the Primos, the stage where the crime took place.

As of now, I have exposed how my career came to be and I have given a bit of insight about some of the characters that would be involved in my daily life. However, starting now I will now be giving the full details on the points of interests related to the case and all its participants, starting by engaging with the officers of the Law who were of immense assistance in apprehending the true criminal.

Chapter 4

3rd Moon

26th Phase

2018

10:49 am

As we drove towards our destination, I took the liberty of reviewing a few of the notes I had taken during my classes, briskly glancing at the fundamentals of criminal investigation. As I contemplated the information, however, I did notice my companion nonchalantly playing with a butterfly knife in his own mindful manner. As frank as I may be, I am not one to be particularly fond of creating small talk with strangers, even less when they present themselves to be somewhat of a loner. However, I will admit that he was a case that had piqued my curiosity, so I could not help but feel strangely attracted to him.

"You're staring awfully hard there," he perceived.

//Ah!//

"M-my apologies! It is just... I am quite fascinated by how someone like yourself is described as the Ace of the Agency, despite looking younger than me."

"Is that so?"

Retracting his knife, he directed his complete attention towards me.

"Hm! As the nature of the work we do, looks can be deceiving. I was brought to be familiar with this line of work since I was young. Director Aether -the one in charge of the Agency- took notice of my abilities once upon a time and decided to enlist me, honing my skills in the process."

//But surely there is more to it than that, right?//

"However, titles mean nothing to me. I welcome the praise, but more than anything I just enjoy solving a good problem, especially the ones that are presented with limited information. But I enough about me, I rather I spend my time giving you a preface to the case, for we're soon arriving at the crime scene."

Picking up his pocketbook, he skimmed through the contents until he found the notes he wished to share.

"Case #167," he began his exposition, "the murder took place on the 24th phase of the 3rd moon at 9:04 pm. The victim's name is Victor Primo, headmaster of the House of Primos, located in the Monchester Villas. He was single, had no next of kin, and was nearing his seventies. According to some of his employees, he had an upcoming meeting with our accused that was scheduled to be around 10:00 pm. Considering he had some time to kill, he decided to watch the evening news while he drank a herbal tea he had been prepared. Having a look at the time. He hurriedly went towards his office, preparing for their arrival. This was the last time anyone saw him alive. The maid went to the kitchen and began preparing a medicine for the headmaster, for he had a terrible stomachache during the day, and she was to make it for him before he went to sleep. The butler, on the other hand, was making sure that everything was fastened up, readily secured in case any intruders decided to storm the estate. Fifteen minutes pass and the maid finishes the medicine, to which she then decided to go upstairs and give it o him. Knocking to announce her arrival, she entered the office and was met with the ghastly view: The body of Victor Primo, dead, taken aback on the floor, slashed from the neck up and stabbed 3 times."

"From the neck up?" I asked.

"Yes, the alleged murder weapon was a chef's knife of around thirty-two. Prints have been dusted off and they seem to belong to Primo's personal lawyer and sous-chef Mr. Jeffrey Hoper. He had been working for the headmaster for the last seven years and had been on good terms with the headmaster."

"But if this Mr. Hoper had been on good terms with the headmaster, what reason would there be for the killing? Is there an established motive at least?"

"Concretely no. As I mentioned before, the butler had made sure that every entrance was fastened. He did not spot anyone approach the house nor any signs that pointed towards an intruder. Naturally, this shows that the culprit must have been already inside, someone who was familiar with the staff -as to not raise suspicion- and the layout of the. The staff had confirmed their own alibis during that night, some returning to their homes and others still working. Regretfully, however, Hoper had no one to confirm his alibi, with him being the last person who was with the headmaster."

//Poor Mr. Hoper, everything just seems to be pointing towards the fellow.//

"But those are the facts as of right now. I'm confident that as we continue our investigation, everything will become clear to us. Speaking of clear, the estate should come into view in this next corner on your right. There it is."

The estate proved to be one to marvel at. It was a two-story building that was accompanied by a bountiful field filled with flora and small decorations, completely surrounded by an iron gate. The architecture was one that gave the impression that it had stood on this land for some years while having a few modern touches done to it to give it a welcoming atmosphere. It was archaic but familiar, if that makes sense. But none of that compares to how wonderful the garden looked like. It was filled with all sorts of flowers, ranging from the Amani frontiers like the gladiolus and blood lilies to the Tōsō planes with roses and orchids. It was accompanied by a medium sized fountain that poured its streaming water to a pond filled with lotus flower.

As I finished surveying the estate, I noticed two vehicles parked in the driveway where I could spot some words pasted on the bumper of each vehicle. It read: 'Bogshire Police Bureau'. These were most surely governmental officers that were assigned to work on the case. As I continued to look, I caught a glimpse of a pair standing in the driveway, possibly keeping bystanders and reporters from the crime scene. One of them was a gruff, broad-shouldered gentleman while the other seemed to be more of a lanky, small bean.

"This is the Primo Residence rook and as of right now, our investigation will begin. I have been assigned to lead the investigation, but I want you to pay attention to your surroundings. Testimony, evidence, accounts, everything. Observe and absorb everything that you possibly can. Any data is good data, no matter how irrelevant it may seem at first glance."

Despite accepting to help in this case, I was still nervous, for I had not expected to start working on a case as soon as my first day. Truthfully, I just did not want to slow him or anyone down.

Taking notice, he gave a soft sigh and turned his gaze towards me.

"Look, don't think about it too much. I'm not expecting you to solve this case from the get-go. I'm not heartless, but I expect our coworkers to be competent. So ong as you do what you've been instructed to do, you'll be fine, I promise."

At his kind words, I was able to collect my composure. With a tight grip on my messenger bag, I mustered up my resolve.

"Right! I won't let you down!" I exclaimed with energy.

"Hm, good. Then we're off."

With an affirming nod, I followed his lead and exited the vehicle, making our way towards the gate. As we walked inside, I asked if he had received any new updates from the officers since this morning.

"No, nothing to speak of for now. The police have made decent progress, but I fear they are not progressing fast enough. It's been more than a day and the investigation seems to have stayed in a limbo. Tell me, from what you gathered from the Agency, what is our professional relationship?"

"Well," I replied frankly, "is it not to work with the officers and shine a light towards the truth?

Allegro groaned audibly, cringing at what I shared with my embarrassment.

"As cliché as those sounds, you aren't necessarily wrong. However, try to go a bit more beyond that."

Giving it some thought, I gave my response.

"Well, private investigators are not exactly allowed to go to any crime scenes without governmental permission. Being ourselves a private company, I would think we function the same way. Helping the officers achieve results quicker with the authority of the government and the ingenuity of the agency."

"Good answer. A general idea, but suffice with what you know. We aren't allowed to investigate crimes relating to murder, theft or kidnapping unless we cooperate with the government. As private investigators, our job is to take a different approach on the matter and offer insight. It can be sharing information from external and non-ethical means, or it can be information that may prove too obvious for the normal eye. A lie begets another lie, so it's our job to find out the source."

"Then, if we are working with them? Why have they not found anything yet?"

"Because they tend to limit their peripheral vision to what they can see instead of what they cannot. I believe that when it comes to criminal investigations, some creativity is always good for the mind. Thinking like how a criminal works and how I would attract the least attention has been one of my many favorite techniques since forever when it comes to solving criminal cases. Fascinating stuff if I may be honest, thanks in part to the training I received by the Director. "

I was surprised by the passion he showed when speaking of his methods. Mr. Allegro has shown to be a person who would rather keep to himself instead of socializing, like a cat who is being approached by several children only to run away with haste. Despite that, his face displayed vigor and life, being the opposite of how he was earlier. Taking notice, he coughed and quickly dissuaded his exuberance to approach his known cold demeanor.

"But I ramble... fundamentally our job is to give them a nudge towards the right direction. For now, though, introduce yourself to those officers."

"W-what?! You are going leave me? Why?"

" I have to make a important call first before I continue where I left off. I'll make sure to reconvene with you as soon as I'm done though. If you'll excuse me."

//Are you serious? What kind of superior leaves their subordinate alone on their first day of the job? Good grief. Well, might as well and just introduce myself and see where it takes me from there, I suppose.//

Although a bit apprehensive, I decided to follow his instructions and make my way towards the familiar pair of officers. Their attire was a black bullet-proof vest, some brown khaki pants combined with a red dress shirt, clearly their defining features being their size and accents. Becoming wary of me, they eyed me with curiosity, to which I then introduce myself to melt away the tension.

"G-greetings! My name is Jennifer Hawkins, and I am an agent of the Collective Detective Agency. I suppose you would not mind if I were to examine the scene from the inside, yes?"

They both gave a suspicious looking face towards my direction and looked towards themselves as if seeking to find an answer to this stranger in front of them.

"I heard of no Hawkins being part of the investigation, have you Charles?" spoke the small man.

"No Michael, I have not!" responded the skinny officer.

"Oh, well, I actually started today. I am an intern, you see, and I was just giving my clearance identification. I trust this ID would be enough for access? I was brought by Mr. Allegro to help assist with the investigation today. I am sure you know of him, yes?"

"Of course we do, why wouldn't we? However, while I do say the ID does look authentic, we can't exactly allow you to enter without running it by with her.

"Aye. Without her approval, we can't allow anyone to enter. Protocols will be protocols and all that."

""Mhm, not even Mr. Allegro is allowed to investigate the scene if he doesn't have her approval, miss, and he is on the VIP list, so to speak."

"I see."

//Pity, I wanted to see the scene before Allegro got here. Not much I can do, might as well just-//

"Hey, what's the holdup?" a sudden voice appeared within the house.

"Ah! Captain Gushiken!" exclaimed both officers in surprise.

""You boys were supposed to report me the status outside ten minutes ago, and I have yet to receive anything! Don't tell me you forgot AGAIN?"

""N-no we didn't! We were going to let you know! We were just finishing explaining to the missy how she can't enter the crime scene. She claims she was granted permission, but we have yet to hear it from you, captain."

"Is that so?"

She gave such an intimidating stare towards me, so much so that if I did not know beforehand that she was the captain, you would have me believe she was some sort of delinquent. She was a woman of a small stature, excluding the black boots she wore. She spoke with an accent that came from overseas, from Tōsō, I believe. She had intense crimson eyes and had silky navy colored hair that shined, giving it a somewhat purple glow. She wore an officer's coat, some suspenders, a small black dress tie over her white dress shirt and some black pants, combining the whole set. She also sported two earrings. On the left, what seemed to be a chained clipped piercing, while on the right a star shaped one. A choker was also visible as well.

"And who might you exactly be? I didn't exactly get a call saying that a scruffy amateur was playing detective around these parts."

"My apologies. I can understand the confusion. My name is Jennifer Hawkins, and I was assigned to assist the police in the current investigations on the killing of Victor Primo. I have my ID here so you can see for yourself."

"Uh-huh, sure you are," she said in a dismissing tone, "listen, I frankly don't give a damn who sent you or who you are. As far as I'm concerned, you're just another bystander playing peepin' tom."

"I'm afraid I lack understanding."

"Do you have a badge?"

"N-no I do not."

"Hired Help papers? Written Authorization by the BPB? If you don't have any of those props, then get out. We already have enough of a headache with the people trying to look and the idiots trying to write an article by getting in the middle of our work. So please, make like a leaf and fly to wherever you came from, or I'll arrest you on obstruction of justice."

Her despicable attitude towards me was exhausting me. All I wanted to do was offer my assistance to achieve the common goal of catching the perpetrator and yet it feels as if I am the person in question.

//What a pain, I am not getting anything done and any further intent to change her mind will prove bad on my end. Maybe I should just go.//

"Were you just planning on leaving? But we haven't even scratched the surface of this case!"

"Mr. Allegro!"

"Well, look who decided to show up."

"Gushi," he nodded. "I apologize, Hawkins, that I took a bit of time, but I'm finally back. Now! Despite the lack of hospitality, it would seem you guys have been well acquainted with Ms. Hawkins. She's a victorian who we had recruited to work with us as an intern. You will see that everything is accounted for and signed by the Director here. I called ahead to your boss and notified him of her inclusion towards the investigation. You will see that I have the authorization here, albeit in a pdf format, which is more than enough if you ask me. I must admit, however, that you have disappointed me with your attitude. Is there really a reason to treat anyone like that, even if they're of a meek appearance?

//Did I look that bad...//

Waving her hand, she disregarded his comments.

"Dude, I don't give a damn. You know I can't exactly be letting anyone near the crime scene. How else was I supposed to act if someone came here claiming to be a detective with no official identification? And I thought I told you to stop calling me Gushi Lucio! Its Captain Gushiken!"

I was left dumbfounded by their interactions. The prickly and fired up captain had become flushed quickly as soon as Mr. Allegro appeared. I sense some history, but I should leave that train of thought for some other time.

"Now then, seeing everything is in order, I assume there won't be any more problems, will there?"

""Tch, no but..."

She sighed and followed her thought.

"Yeah, fine whatever. This is irregular, but considering that everything is filled, I'm not gonna complain."

"Thank you for understanding," he smiled warmly, "don't worry though, I'll still be leading the investigation with you. She's just going to be assisting us."

She gave a look towards me and I instinctively bowed with respect.

"I will do my best. I look forward to working with you!" I said.

She gave a hearty sigh and finally gave me her authorization.

Very well. Welcome to the team. The name's Holly Gushiken, Police Captain of the Governmental Police Force under the Bogshire Police Bureau."

Nodding, her officers saluted welcomed me with a salute.

"Now, Hawkins, was it? Before anything, I'd like to apologize for my attitude earlier. I just get worked up by all things in regard to meddlers and reporters trying to get inside crime scenes unauthorized. The least I can do for a newbie like you is to let you know on what we have. So what do you know so far?"

I explained to her on what I had learned so far.

"Yeah, that's the gist of it. Lucio here was helping us find anything that seemed to be of interest. We managed to find the murder weapon, and the witnesses are accounted for on the night in question. We believe that Mr. Jeffrey Hoper -who has been taken into custody and taken to the Detention Center- was the one who did the crime. Our boys and I believe that it was him and he's going to be charged with first degree murder."

"If I may, on what ground exactly is Mr. Hoper being charged for?"

"We were going to actually speak of that with Lucio when he got here. Me and the boys did some digging, and we found that there has been some history between the two men."

The captain pulled some notes out of her pocket.

"Truth is, this Mr. Hoper had worked as a consultant for the victim for some time. He would present his case towards Mr. Hoper, seeking some advice, be it financial or legal. He is an attorney you see, and he was a damn good one. I'll tell you that much. He studied abroad in the country of Tōsō for seven years. With a mind as bright as his, it was a no-brainer on why the victim decided to enlist him in his staff, paying him a total of six hundred deidras a week, a very generous pay, if you will. You might ask why instead of pursuing a full job as a lawyer -since he had received a lot of invitations to work in various firms- he decided to work with the headmaster. Well, the reason was that they had both developed an affectionate relationship. So much so that Mr. Primo never feared of leaving Mr. Hoper alone in the house or even being alone with the lad. So much so that he made him sous chef of the house. In a manner of weeks, he mastered the craft. He was so good in the kitchen that even the head chef showed signs of frustrations, for he feared his job was in danger of being lost. That's at least what the employees said, anyway."

If I may, what was the chef's name? I asked.

"Relevance?"

"I take it upon myself to write any note I can, no matter how insignificant they might be."

"Heh, excellently well put, Hawkins. Holly, you and I both know that any data is good data no matter how small it may be."

Chief Gushiken shrugged.

"If you say so. His name is Richard McKenzie. We haven't gotten the chance to talk with him yet. He should be staying with his wife in his home in Sunset Hills. You're more than welcome to talk to him if you find him, so long as you give his account to us."

"Thank you, you may continue Gushi."

She gave a disgusted, disapproving look.

"Anyway, all seemed to go well for the lad. The afternoon before the murder, however, seemed to say the opposite. A loud outburst had been exchanged between the two. It lasted for some time until after a while it was dead quiet. Growing worried, one of them decided to check up on them and it was then that they came across the body, the deed already done."

"Does anyone know what is it that was being discussed?"

"Frustratingly no, we have no idea what matters where being talked about. Not even Hoper wants to talk about it.

However, considering that the man was in heat, me and the lads have concluded that in a fit of rage, he retrieved his personal kitchen knife to kill him off. Yeah, we interviewed a few of the witnesses and they told us that the knife in question was his personal work knife when he was working in the kitchen. The fact that the slash was followed with three stab wounds clearly proves that it was done on anger, proving that whatever they spoke was something very troubling to the suspect. That is all we have gathered so far, and it is why we requested the Agency to assist us in confirming the theory, for that is the only possible outcome that has surged out of the altercation and the evidence we have collected."

I jotted this additional information on my personal notepad. The motive might have a foundation, but I still questioned it. if they had built a relationship throughout the years than shouldn't just talking it out end it over? And if could not, what was being discussed that left such a negative impression on Mr. Hoper? Moreover, does the presence of the head chef Richard McKenzie bear any relevance? Might there be something else intertwined in this case? Clearly, these are questions that are in valid need of looking over.

Mr. Allegro, however, grew impatient of the exposition for the police have not made significant progress since the last time they met.

"In other words, there has not been any progress. Wonderful." he replied with snark.

"Well, we would have made more progress, but you decided to disappear from the crime scene to God knows where without telling anyone."

"Does a hound need their owners to sniff a scent? You stare and admonish my ways of finding clues and yet you lack the ingenuity to find some. It's no wonder why the BPB often requests my assistance to help you despite having the audacity to critique my ways."

"Excuse me?"

Tensions began rising as the two sides of the law began a fiery confrontation. The officers were left filled with sighs and exasperations to the point that it looked like they were already used to it.

"R-regardless," I interjected, "we are here now, so if it is alright with you, we would like to investigate the room and assist with any way we can."

Growing calm by my remark, she nodded in agreement.

"Yeah, sure. You've been very respectful to us, and you've been given permission to help us, so I don't see why not you shouldn't. However, if you do find something, make sure you share it as soon as you can. There's always an off chance that our train of logic has gone sideways, so we wish to correct it anyway we can so that no innocent person becomes jailed from wrongful accusations. The room in question is on the second floor down the hall to your right. If you ever need any help, just ring one of my boys."

"You will not be joining us?"

"Nah, I gotta fill some paper works regarding our progress at the moment. Here is a copy of all the notes and information we have collected as well as some photos we took before taking the body to the coroner. Anything else? No? Well, good luck then."

Giving us they all the information they have gathered, she exits the estate and drives towards her destination southbound from where we stood.

Chapter 5

3rd Moon

26th Phase

2018

12:01 pm

Having been granted access to investigate, we decided to make our way towards the office, where the crime occurred. The space resembled a classic Victorian style interior, where the wallpaper and baseboard played around the walls. Navy was the color of choice, with hints of brown complementing the overall color scheme the designer had in mind when designing the room. A solitary art piece rested on the southern wall of the room, a self-portrait done by the headmaster himself. As a result, by the struggle, contraptions and knickknacks littered the ground, with only a bellow camera standing tall.

The Victorian furniture was disarranged, and it was evident that a struggled had occurred by both parties. In the middle, a small chandelier loomed over the room, giving it a warm light that exposed the tape that reconstructed how the body was found. The body had been moved to the coroner with the intention of finding the cause of death, the time of death and any other evidence that would give us insight into the crime.

The blood was still left faint on the wooden floor, possibly as a result from the slashes on his neck, for no other source was found as reported by the given officers. "A struggle seemed to have happened," I pointed out. "The furniture shows signs of slight movement while some mark prints can be observed upon close inspection." "You are correct. If we consider the testimony from the employees to be true, it is obvious to conclude that a heated discuss on was indeed taking place prior to the killing, arousing suspicion towards the accused." "Right. It would be prudent then to speak with Mr. Hoper once we are done investigating here.

After all, if he is to be innocent, then why not be completely honest with the officers? "Yes, that is the question. However, there are times people would rather keep their mouth shut than speak at all. Which is why it is our job to crack open the answers." "I guess so. But still, I believe that being honest can save you from even more trouble, no matter how hard or bad it might be for you. Regretfully, this just makes the case against him stronger." "So, you believe he is innocent as well?" "I do. Does it not sound nonsensical that after all those years of service, he suddenly became a monster and killed his employer?

Usually, when there is more than one act of aggression done upon a body, it signifies that a grudge had been ensnared upon the perpetrator. And while yes, they appeared to be at odds the last time they spoke, I do not think that one would suddenly betray their trust over a single disagreement. No, I think something else is afoot." "Hm, is that so?" Smiling with intrigue, he chuckled softly at my line of thought. "Professionally cautious or optimistically chanceful?

I'll admit, your line of thought isn't all that far-fetch with what we already know. However, until we can find something that disproves his involvement completely, there's not much we can do for now. I will advise you for now, though, to jot down those points you mentioned and return to them once we discuss them with the accused." "Very well," I responded. After carefully examining the rest of the room, I decided to inspect the bellow camera in all its detail.

"It would seem Mr. Primo was a collector of sorts." He picked up his notes and located the tab regarding the information of Primo. "He was an avid collector of antiquities, and he often made his trips around the world finding pieces of interest. This bellow camera, for example, is a mk.1K variation from the 1800s." "mk.1k? I do not think that's a version I have not heard before." "You wouldn't. It's a prototype never taken to the public market. It was deemed too unstable for use. They had them returned and made some variations of the original: mk. 2K, mk.3K and mk.4K. Those are the generic ones you come to be more familiarized with regard to vintage bellow cameras. Now as to how he achieved to obtain this prototype is beyond me."

"Could he possibly have gotten it from someone who worked on it?" I asked curiously. "Highly doubt it. This isn't something you would be able to obtain by normal means. If I had to guess, it could have been by an underground auction he had won a long time ago. The origin bears no relevance so don't think about it too much. Instead of focusing on how he obtained it, focus on the camera. There's a clue there that even the officers have overlooked." Taking his suggestion to heart, I decided to inspect the camera and all the nook and crannies it presented itself with. I did not find anything noteworthy. "I could not find anything. It just seems like a regular camera to me."

"Give it another look. Try to go the extra mile with your observation." Inspecting it once more, I did not find what my companion was referring to. "I would appreciate it if you could shine a light for me," I remarked. Thinking of a way to nudge me in the right direction, he followed with a question. "Tell me what do you know about dust?" "Dust?" "Yes, dust." "Just the basics. It is something that naturally forms in the surrounding atmosphere. It comes from natural items such as rocks and dirt as well as dead skin cells."

"Correct. Now, while the staff does it's best to have the house in its best conditions, you can observe that dust is starting to collect. On the floor, on the furniture, so on and so forth. And yet on this singular camera there is a spot that seems to lack any of it." "Ah! I see now! Someone must have touched the device!" "Correct. Although the spot in question is relatively small, I believe that some sort of fingerprint must have been left behind by the culprit." "Extraordinary!" I exclaimed. "We should notify the officers so they can analyze it as soon as possible!" "That won't be necessary."

"What? But do we not need their assistance to find out who the prints belong to?" "Have you forgotten who you are working for? We have our own equipment that helps us on our investigations, more so than what any of those grounded officers have." I could not seem to comprehend what he meant with that. Confused, I watched as my companion directed his attention towards the ring he had on his ring finger. With a touch to it, a voice came about. "Hello! What can I do for you?" said a small voice.

"Dawn, I need you to analyze these marks left on the camera. See if you can pull any fingerprints." "Of course! Commencing analysis." Once his conversation ended, he moved his fist towards the camera .I was confused, for I had not understood who he was talking to nor what he was doing. I assumed it was a sort of communicator, so I paid no mind. But after some time, the voice came back. "Analysis complete! After an extensive scan on the designated spot, I could not identify any fingerprints left behind." "Huh! this keeps proving to be interesting, " he said with delight in his voice. "No fingerprints then? Oh bother, what a waste."

"On the contrary! It only proves something else entirely." "How so?" "Think about it. A mark was left on the camera, and yet there were no prints detected." I grew into thought, but the only thing that came to mind was something painful. Surely you do not mean to believe that there was a third person. And for that matter, someone had burned them to not be traced? "But of course! I think it would be logical to conclude to that." "With all due respects that sounds absurd."

"Does it? Fingerprints are left behind every time we touch something. That is the nature of it. If you, the officers, Gushiken, Hoper or even the victim for that matter, had touched the device, then there would be results. But that is not the case. So, it's sound to conclude that someone was here before or during the killing." "Besides," he pointed towards the glass window, "if you take a look outside of the window, you'll see signs of an intruder as well."

//Signs?//

At his suggestion, I opened the window and looked around. It was then that I noticed that the rose bushes below were disturbed, the roses crushed by what seemed to be a drop of weight." "By Jove!", I cried. "Still think there wasn't another person involved? Hoper couldn't have done that that much is certain. And no one spotted this ghost despite evidence suggesting that there was someone here in fact. Hm, if my intuition is correct then this mystery is taking a turn towards a most complicated matter."

With this introspective, this theory proved to be a possibility. 'The lack of evidence proves to be the evidence' was the lesson he was teaching me. Furthermore, the evidence of the bushes proved to support the idea he had suggested. And, while it id sound absurd the moment he shared that, I had to admit that the more I thought about it, the more it started to become was a very convincing line of thought. "Perhaps you may be right. It would be prudent to keep this in mind then. From the look of it though, I do not think there is anything here left investigating. Might there be another area around the room worth looking over?"

"Not particularly, no. We've already done our work here for today here." "Then I suggest that we head towards the Detention Center and speak with Mr. Hoper, seeing we have a few things we need to talk about." "And that is?" he asked testing me. "First, to hear from him what it was they spoke of. Understanding it could help us find if he really had a motive to do the killing. Secondly, to confirm if there was indeed a third person or not. If there was indeed another party in the room, then that opens the possibility for the events to be interpreted in a different way, a way that not even the officers are even aware of. And then there is the nature of the bellow camera.

Perhaps he might offer insight on the device and why it was tampered with." Mr. Allegro showed signs of being visibly impressed with everything I have showed since we started investigating. "Well, you're coming along quite nicely. You have already identified the point of interest and you seem to be gaining confidence in the procedure. If you keep this up, then you'll become a professional in no time. Now come, let us be off and take the apple straight from the horse's mouth." With that, we began making our way towards the local detention center, where Mr. Hoper was being detained until yesterday morning.

My companion called the captain to ask permission to speak with the accused. She allowed us to speak with him so long an officer was present during the interview. Making the arrangements she hangs up and we march towards the Detention Center. Deciding to offer some conversation, I ask him about his connection towards the Captain. "I observe that some history is shared between Ms. Gushiken and you," I comment curiously. "Who's to say." "Well, for starters, it is not normal to call someone by a nickname, especially during work duties." "On the contrary, I think it is fine to give a sort of nickname to people. It builds trust and comradery between one and another.

Besides, I was never one to be fussy regarding what people should address me so in return I do the same. Does this bear any relevance to the case?" "Not particularly. I was just curious for as to the type of relationship you two had. I noticed that there was some familiarity between the two." "The only familiarity I have with her is her need to constantly get in my way. Ugh, don't get me wrong, she's as sharp as they make them, and her courage is what officers look up to. But she's just too stubborn. You could create the greatest argument ever and that would never be enough to make her consider it. If there is no physical evidence, she won't pay attention to you. She would rather die on a hill than adapt her reasoning with some creative exercises."

"It would seem you do know a lot about her." "And it would seem you prefer to ask a lot about unimportant things.'

//Ah!//

"R-right. My apologies." He gave a very audible sigh and collected his composure. "In any case, you can see why finding evidence is critical important in this line of work. Ah, we're here. Come, let us find the accused." As we entered we were welcomed by the lovely receptionist, who greeted us with delight. "Good afternoon! How can I help you?" "Good day. My name is Lucio Allegro of the CDA and I'm here with my assistant Ms. Hawkins. We have an interview planned with the accused regarding the Primo case. If you could direct us towards the holding cell, we would greatly appreciate."

"Of course! The Captain told us about you two. We have made the arrangements, so when you're ready be sure to go to the officer next to the entrance." "Right, thanks." Upon the lobby officer's direction, we made our way towards the cell. Our escort mentioned that we only have thirty minutes to work with and that if it proved to get too out of control he would interfere if necessary. Consenting towards the protocols, he opens the gate for us and we managed to enter the cell. It was a pitiful scene what we saw. What came before us was a man sitting on the corner of the cell hopelessly exhausted of all that has happened to him. If it was not enough for him that he, was he was being treated as the prime suspect, then surely the death of his friend must have had a toll on him for the last days. He was a man that looked close to his 30s.

He dressed in a business casual fashion, a white dress shirt tuckered under his square shaped brown pants and a lone red colored tie giving it a bit of life. He was particularly skinny, and his features were even more accentuated for it looked like he has not eaten anything for the past few days. He presented some facial hair, and his hair was kept, although the sweat of the brow has clearly made it more disarranged.

He was shaken. "Excuse me, might you be esquire Hoper?" my companion asked. "Who's asking? I already told everything I knew this morning..." "My friend, we are not police officers. My name is Lucio Allegro. I am a private investigator from the Collective Detective Agency, and this is my assistance, Jennifer Hawkins." "Good day." "Oh. so, your people from that Agency then. Well... either way, I already told them what I know. You're just wasting your time. Sorry." "Well, that is for us to decide. There are a few questions we would like answered regarding some new information we have obtained. We would appreciate it if you cooperated with us."

"And... that is?" "We would like to know what exactly you discussed with the victim." Mr. Hoper became visibly distraught at his inquiry. "What is there to talk about? I am not in a position to disclose any confidentiality with my clients, even if they have passed on. " "We believe, Mr. Hoper, that the key to this mystery lies in your answers. The simple fact is that the victim died as soon as your confrontation ended and right now, you're the prime suspect. Between the lack of alibi and the murder weapon, everything seems to just point towards you."

He gave a long look and mumbled a few words I managed to pick up: "So, it really is the end for me." Truthfully, he was on such a pity state. Even though we did not have the evidence at the moment, you could clearly see in his eyes that he knew nothing to do with the killing. I read on my studies that often people are wrongfully accused. Be it by planted evidence, contradicting accounts or just bad luck, cases like these tend to cause an error in judgement on behalf of the detectives. But seeing that was the case with him, made me feel compassion for the poor fellow.

"The truth is we personally do not believe you did the crime. We believe in your innocence, and it is our job to prove it." "You do? Why?" "Because we feel there is more to it than what we know right now. And, if you were the killer, I do not think you would be suffering as you are now. In any case, you would just be asking for a lawyer. However, we need your help if we are to clear your name and find the person who did it. Please, if you could just share us a few minutes of your time, we would greatly appreciate it."

He gave us a despondent look and remained still. I was starting to grow anxious, for time was not on our side and our only lead was turning to be a lost one. "If you don't want to talk to us, then alright." interjected Mr. Allegro. "But let me ask you one question before we leave: During the time this meeting took place where you both accompanied by a third individual? He gave a hesitation, and, with a fidget in his eyes, he answered. No. No, there was not another soul in that room." My colleague gave a quiet chuckle.

"Truly. It is unfortunate that even when we are giving our services towards your innocence, you have yet to be truthful. Miss Hawkins, if you may." Following to where he was going for, I took out the pictures taken from my polaroid and exhibited them towards the accused. "What am I supposed to be looking at exactly? Is that not the camera of Mr. Primo"

"Tell me, my companion asked, did the late headmaster ever use this device?" "Not that I recall, no. I was told that such a device is treated as a family heirloom and, under no circumstances, is anyone allowed to touch it." "Right, so if he did not use it, then we can conclude that it's been left off in a state of unused. And yet it would seem not everyone followed this strict rule. See for yourself." "Hm? Wait, is that?!"

"It would seem you already are aware. Indeed, some marks had been left off."

Mr. Hoper became visibly alarmed at the revelation. "This is absurd!" he cried. "Who would dare to touch the device that we were specifically told to leave be?" "Who would indeed? That is the question. Might you have a guess?" "No!" he exclaimed. "Everyone who works at the house are pure saints. They did their job as they were told. If someone were to leave marks, then they would have most certainly been an outsider!" With that, my companion gave a glance towards me, confidant that his intuition was right.

"Then it would seem thar I was right. Indeed, it is just like you said. Current evidence suggests that someone had indeed tampered with the device. Naturally, it could not have been the late headmaster. He was a very plump fellow, for he had thick stubby hands, whereas the mark left on the device was that of a skinny individual, more bone than mass. And, while you're indeed a slim gentleman, you would never do such a thing. Knowing the respect you had for him, a thought like that would never cross your mind." Mr. Hoper's eyes were twinkling at this exposition. He was shocked but in awe, for he had witnessed the genius of Mr. Allegro. Like a conductor and his symphony, he masterfully executed his logical conclusion to the point that not even the older gentleman could counter. And if I am to be honest, I was also visibly impressed. We had just met today, and I have been already enchanted by his performance during our time together.

//Spectacular. So this is the ace of the Agency them.//

"There is no use thinking of excuse. No. I think it is high tide you started being honest." He began to think it through, for the gentleman knew there really was no other way to be dodgy about it. He pondered and pondered, and after a while, he knew what he had to do. He took some deep breaths and finally decided to talk. "Very well. I guess it won't make a difference if I start lying. It is as you say, there was someone else in the room."

"Who is it then?" "His name is Frederick Facsimile. He is an old family acquaintance of the Primos. I have not exactly been told all the details, but he already had a history with Victor. Not even my great friend -may he rest in peace- shared all the intricacies. What I am aware of is that Frederick had been working with my friend for more than fifteen years and that during that period, they had developed a sort of respect for one another.

He was Victor's secretary, you see. Diligent and focused on details, he garnered respect from the house and there was no other person who my friend trusted with his own life during that period. But if I should be honest -since that is what that you are asking of me- I never once trusted the bloke. No, behind his fake smile, I always had the feeling that he was only nice to my friend to achieve something greater."

"Despite his treatment towards the headmaster, he never once treated our colleagues with the same respect. He looked down upon everyone and I would care to think he never once liked me. Bitterness and anger were all I ever saw in his eyes. Was it because of my friendship with the headmaster? Or was it because I never once showed him the respect, he demanded from everyone? I am not sure. But I digress. I have told you everything I know. I only wish that I was of service, for you have clearly shown that you are being of service to my time of need."

"Interesting! he exclaimed. "Very, very interesting. I take it then that he was the person who touched the device?" "Of course not! Mr. Facsimile was a very sour character to be sure, but he always did his job and never considered disobeying any rule. His job would be on the line if he had done so. Besides, he was sitting next to me, so he had no way of reaching the device. How those prints were left is beyond me, but I can assure you none of us were the person responsible for it." "I see! Just one last thing. Did the victim have any enemies.

Any people at all that would have reason to kill him?" "No. Not that I can think of. The man was a solitary person. Other than his employees, he would prefer to keep himself away from society. He was a kind, generous person who treated those that were in his life with kindness. He placed others ahead of him and would often treat us like we were a part of his family. I can speak for everyone when I say that it has been difficult for all of us. And to think that the last thing I did was fight with him..."

//Mr. Hoper...//

"I understand. I won't press any further. I appreciate the time you have shared with us I'll make sure to let you know how our investigation is going next time we have the chance to speak. Now, if you'll excuse us." "Are you leaving?" "Afraid so. We have some business to attend to and our time is up."

"Oh, I see." "Just hold on for a little while longer until we get to the bottom of this. We are going to get you out of this. It is only a matter of time. Okay?"

"I understand." "Good! Then we're off. Hawkins let's go." "Right. Let us be-" "Thank you!" interjected Mr. Hoper. "Hm?" "Knowing that the case is being handled by the right hands puts me at ease. More than my own imprisonment, I just want every one of my colleagues safe and my fallen friend avenged. And more than anything, I appreciate you two believing in me." "Of course! In the end, we just want to help, so it is the least we can do." "He-he of course. Farewell then."

Chapter 6

3rd Moon

26th Phase

2018

1:40 pm

"Well, what do you make of that, Hawkins?" asked my companion.

"That you were right, and that there were indeed more people besides the victim and suspect. Between what we found on the crime scene and his testimony, it is safe to conclude that there is a third witness and possibly a fourth."

"Naturally. And if this Facsimile presents some prints on his hands, which I'm inclined to think he does, will prove that someone altogether was present on the scene of the crime. Possibly our real killer."

"Perhaps. Even so, if we assume this fourth member was the person who landed on the bush you spotted, -with such a high altitude, if I might add- we can say that we are not dealing with an average criminal."

"Indeed. No sane person would dare to remove their prints unless for a reason. Plus, seeing the room was left spotless, it goes to show you that we're dealing with something else entirely."

Writing down the draft of our findings, I then gave a look at the time, seeing if we had time to continue where we left off.

"It is half-past three at the moment and I believe we still have time to speak with the culinarian. Hearing his account of the affair could prove beneficial."

"That would be wise. I messaged the CDA to locate Facsimile so discussing with this culinarian should prove good use of our time now. Gushi mentioned that he's living in Sunset Hills. Traffic starts coming around this time, so we should pick up the pace."

The ride was of great length. To pass the time, we engaged in conversation. Considering that I have not spent much time in the country since I got here, Mr. Allegro gave a history about Bogshire. To my surprise, he showed extensive knowledge, but the content proved to be too much and uninteresting for me, that I mostly just daydreamed on the trip. So, I will do the favor to whoever reads this and skip it.

"But anyway, that's a general idea of the history of the country. Rather interesting, is it not?" he finished accounting.

"Hm? O-oh yeah! Very interesting stuff!"

//And here I thought wasn't going to finish.//

"'The country founded on wars.' An intimidating title to be sure, but an abandoned one. Bogshire has evolved from its origins, now partaking in the art of the trade. Fast forward today and you're living in the world center of market trading, where people from different cultures come to do business. Because of it, they left in the past all its violent origins and began acting more civilized and amiable. Between the thriving economy, the status as a central hub and the country's neutrality on many political matters, Bogshire has achieved peace between its neighboring nations."

"I see," I feigned interest.

"Right?", he smiled, "Nothing like a common goal can't do, especially when even to this day they still manage to be as free as can be with no single person in control. While there really is no person with power over the country, a system does do its best to keep the nation in check. It is by that reason that a cabinet was formed, filled with over 100 members. But I digress. I was not one to enjoy talking about politics, so I'd rather stop here. Ah, but we're finally here."

A medium-sized house sat peacefully as the smoke from the chimney flew up towards the heavens. It was a beautiful day, and if it was not because I was working at the moment, a picnic would have been perfect for this scenery.

"When it comes to dealing with potential witnesses, we must always treat them with kindness. We risk losing information if our choice of words does not reflect our demeanor. And above all, never question too hard on them. The least we need is making them clam up and feeling like a suspect. There's a reason why I always try to be as kind as possible to everyone. Irrelevant information is better than no information. Now, let us meet our witness."

With a knock on the solid oak door, some footsteps could be heard from the inside. Finding who the knocking guests were, she opened the door, and we were greeted by a tall, elegant woman with curly mid length hair. She introduced herself as Matilda, the wife of Mr. McKenzie. We gave her a brief explanation of our visit and how we needed to speak with him with regard to the sudden case we were working on.

"We have no suspicion of your husband, madam," I kindly assured her. "We just wish to talk with your husband to a few points of interests he might be aware of."

My companion gave a nod.

"If you're worried about your husband and his role in this case, don't be. As my partner just said, we have no reason to believe he was the killer, or an accomplice, for that matter. So long as helps us, there shouldn't be any problems."

After a few seconds of hesitation, she was convinced by our assuring words.

"He is in the backyard tending to his garden at the moment. I am sure he would not mind a few minutes to help you investigators."

"Of course, thank you Mrs. McKenzie."

"Thank you, Miss."

With that, she invited us in and took us to the backyard. Speaking in a foreign language, I would assume she was notifying him that he had some visitors. With a look towards his shoulder, he signaled to his wife to invite us to his back-yard and continued his work. It was a truly bountiful sight. Crops like corn and wheat were made in abundance while berry shrubs and tomato plants were growing hastily, almost in time for the harvest, for it was the season where they produced their best fruits.

"Favorable time to engage in cultivation, isn't it?" interjected my companion. "The temperatures are just right about there to make them grow. Surely with some local fertilizer and some sunlight, these beautiful plants will produce many wonderful fruits and vegetables, much needed in your area of expertise."

"Da," responded coolly the hardworking man, "Is as you said. Have to make as much progress in this little garden of mine, so that we may keep earning the fruits of our labor, no?" said as he laughed in delight.

As he had finished, he left his hoe near the shed, gently approaching us.

"Pleasure to make your acquaintance. My name is Richard McKenzie. I assume you have come here to speak about Mr. Primo's death, yes?"

He was a short, stout man. Bush browec, ebony haired and sunburnt. He sported a bush well-groomed moustache, complementing his rugged face. He sported a scar right above his right eye, completely blind from it. He dressed in some overalls, a set of gloves and working boots, needed clothes when working with soil and plants. Despite he's somewhat rough appearance, he was very hearty in his way of speaking.

"Yes, we wish to ask a few questions ir regard to the headmaster and the events transpired."

"Cleaning his hands on the nearby basin, he was open to answer any questions.

"Of course, of course! What are you want to know?"

"What were you doing during the night of the murder?" I asked bluntly.

"Hm? Well, I was counting materials for the dishes for the next day. We make an account for all that is to be used. Once I was done, I made my way towards the vehicle to return home. I finished tasks around ten. My comrades can confirm my whereabouts."

"Did you notice anything out of the ordinary before that night?"

"Nyet. Everyone was working in their respective stations. Hoper was working with me for the evening dinner, and the servants were preparing the dining room."

"Speaking of," interjected Mr. Allegro, "a witness mentioned us that you were growing in anger that this up-starter had earned a second job and the favor of the Master. Care to elaborate?"

"Hm, well, this bears no relevance to killing, but I do not think I mind sharing that information. Of course, I was frustrated. If you have been working for more than 30 years to be where you are now and suddenly a young man came and earned the position, would you not feel like that? You would not understand, for you two are as young as they can be. Still, I had nothing against the young man."

"So, you don't believe he could have done the killing?" asked Mr. Allegro.

"God forbids he kills house fly!", he laughed whole-heartedly. "Hoper is a kind lad. No, he would never do such a thing. A little reserved, but earnest in everything. Even assigned as my sous-chef, he always gave me respect and nothing but kindness. Cordial, attentive and open, that itself is the reason why Mr. Primo took an incredible fondness to him. I would be damned if I did not grow to be fond of him. That much is truth."

"Thank you for your honest answers, Mr. McKenzie. I just have one last question. What do you make of Mr. Facsimile? We have been made aware that he had problems with the staff, so we wish to confirm the facts. Could you elaborate?"

He grew silent at the unexpected question. His jovial face was gone, his brow now sunken in.

"I do not know," he answered in a dodgy fashion.

"Come now," uttered Mr. Allegro. "you've been cooperative so far and now you choose to clam up?"

"What is there to say? It is clear you know of his attitude."

"Right. Hawkins, could I talk to you for a second?"

"S-sure."

Pulling me towards the other side of the backyard, I ask what he wanted.

"What is it, sir?'

"It would seem that there is something afoot here."

"Is there? Why would you conclude with that?"

"Do you not see his projection? Despite him not being linked to the case, he doesn't want to answer. That shows that something is preventing him from speaking up. I could press for his reasoning on not answering, but I fear he might grow angry and make matters worse. He doesn't seem like the type of person who would cause the killing or help, for that matter, so I'd rather not include any innocent by-standers. We have our hands full already with Hoper and his predicament."

I grew in thought, finding a way to help Mr. Allegro, for he had done most of the work as of right now. Finding the right words, I return towards the culinarian, speaking my mind in the process.

"Hawkins?"

"Mr. McKenzie," I interjected, "It would do you well if you were to be honest right now. The reason we are here is that we need information. There is a chance you might serve as a key for the case and possibly save what we presume to be an innocent man. If I am to be frank as of this moment, we have no reason to suspect you of murder or being an accomplice. So, for your own sake and your poor wife, we need you to answer us. Please."

He grew despondent and retreated to think it through. After a few short minutes, he returned, half hesitant to give his answer.

"I do not want my poor Matilda to suffer. And yet I do not want her to be in danger as well."

Thinking intently, he considered his options as we waited with patience.

"If I help you, could you promise to take care of Matilda?"

"Now, why would you need our protection?" asked Mr. Allegro.

"Because what I am about to say might put my family in danger."

Surprised, I was left without an answering. Considering his worries, Mr. Allegro nodded and accepted his plea.

"Very well. You have our word."

"Thank you, friend. I'll make sure to keep your word for it then. Very well. There really is no use of hiding anything, for I am sure that both inspectors can figure out why I refuse to answer."

"What of Facsimile then?"

"He gave a visibly disgusted face.

"He is a dastard in all ways of the word. He treated myself with few little compassions and even considered me different just because I am from. We are in 21st century and we still have people like that! His treatment for our comrades was terrible and pretended to be like he was the son of Mr. Primo. The only person who would ever bark back was Mr. Hoper. With how he would never let him get away with his way nor gave the respect he demanded, he was the only one who had won Mr. Facsimile's hatred."

"Hm, is that so? Illuminating for sure. What about the argument Primo and Hoper had? I'm sure you were made aware of that, correct?"

"How could I not? The only thing that has been talked about between staff was that. My concentration on anything was broken because that was the only thing that was being said!"

"Can you confirm that on the house at night nothing could be heard? They mentioned they could hear muffle sounds but not the actual dialogues."

"Da, that is true. The house walls are made with noise cancelling materials. However, if a sound is loud enough, you can faintly hear something. That is the reason why when we announce dinner time we have to go directly to the rooms."

"Do you know what they were going to discuss?"

"Honestly no, I could not. I am never to enjoy eavesdropping on conversations. However, whatever it was must have been something big. Before I finished work, Hoper had gotten out of the room. So, I bid goodnight, but he was too distraught that he was unaware I was there."

"I see. One last question. Was there anyone who had a grudge against the late headmaster?"

McKenzie grew silent, refusing to answer.

"I know I said that I would help if you protected my family, but I feel that this would grow to be even worse for us. If you wish to know, you should go speak with Mr. Facsimile."

//There, he grew silent the moment we asked about Mr. Facsimile again. I am sure Mr. Allegro made the connection.//

"I see now. He was the one who blackmailed you."

He grew silent.

"No matter, I understand fully the position you are in right now. One more question. There was a lone bellow camera in the crime scene. Has that ever been used before?"

"Oh God, no!" exclaimed the rough fellow. "We were made aware of the family history of the camera and how it was valued above anything else. We dared not to touch the dreaded thing. If someone did play with it, then they would surely be fired the moment Primo knew about it."

"I see. It all makes sense now..." he muttered.

"What does?" I asked curiously.

"Hm? Oh, never mind that for now. I thank you for your cooperation even if it putted you in a bind. We will make sure the Agency gives you the protection you both need, Mr. McKenzie."

With an assuring smile, he extended his hands towards Mr. McKenzie. Both gentlemen shaking hands. A deal had been placed.

"That is good to hear, and I apologize for not helping any further. Just make sure you catch the killer, da?"

With that, we bid our goodbyes for the kind couple and continued our journey. As we walked towards our car, I noticed Mr. Allegro growing in thought.

"Have you made sense of anything?" I asked.

"Mm, not yet. I still need a bit more of information before I can infer anything conclusive. However, we can definitely say Facsimile is involved in this somehow, in due part to his blackmailing."

"I figured as much. Mr. McKenzie seemed like a hearty fellow, but as soon as we mentioned his name, his countenance grew a shade of grey each time."

"I agree. Which is why we'll do our other errand and proceed with finally meeting this mysterious fellow."

"I take it you received his location?"

"Naturally. Coincidentally, I've been informed that he's staying in a nearby pub called Ol' Ale. So, it would be prudent to march without delay. Let us see who this Facsimile really is then, shall we?"

Chapter 7

3rd Moon

27th Phase

2018

2:35 pm

A huge sign with the words 'Ol' Ale' sat atop the building. It presented itself as a small two-story building where, up on the porch, fellows were drinking and sharing a game of cards on the tables. Upon entering through the opened doors, the air was filled with the scent of booze and tobacco. Like a betting ring, it was a completely chaotic mess, where our voices were barely audible thanks to the nature of the pub.

"I feel like it will take all afternoon to find our witness with all the people running about here." I remarked."I am inclined to agree. We can either split up to cover more ground or we can call everyone's attention.""Erm, considering we are currently on an investigation, the last thing we need right now is calling attention to ourselves. I suggest we split up."

"Fair point. Then if we're splitting up, please take this."Mr. Allegro reached into his pocket and retrieved a small device, a transmitter of sorts."Put that in your ear. It'll let us stay in touch in case something arises. Take the second floor. I'll stay here in the meantime and speak with some of the regulars and staff to see what I can find.""Got it. I'll be off then."

With that, I made my way towards the stairs as directed by Mr. Allegro. I was introduced to a long corridor, one room to the left and two rooms to the right. Feeling that I should do my utmost best, I began my search for Mr. Facsimile on the left side. The door on the left was wide opened. It was clean and tidy from the inside, possibly arranged by the housekeeper after the tenant had left. The only thing that caught my attention was a clock that had stopped working on the corner wall. It was marked 10:45. Curious, I made a note of this and took a picture in case it might bear relevance later.

As I wrote down this detail, a small object caught my attention. Kneeling, I look below the bed, to which I spotted a small button possibly left by the tenant who had stayed in the room."Curious. Judging by the size, this must have been broken from the cuff of a shirt or blazer." I speak.Realizing that the room had no other features that interested me, I slowly closed the door and tried to make as little noise as possible. Following my inspection, I went to the doors on the right.

The first door had a sign next to it that read 'under renovation'. It was filled with some workers possibly doing their yearly maintenance and quality control services so that the room remains habitable. As for the second door, a vacuum apparatus could be heard from inside, a housekeeper possibly doing her cleaning duties right now.

//I could introduce myself and ask her about Mr. Facsimile's whereabouts. Considering this building is not big to begin with, she might have an idea where he is. But then again, I might not have this opportunity and have access to investigate what I can on this floor without interruptions. No, I think it would be best if I examined everything first before talking with anyone.//

It was a quarter past four, and so far, I have not heard anything from my partner. I was beginning to grow worried, for he was staying in radio silence, not updating me in any way or form. And if it was not bad enough, I was not having the best of luck investigating. The balcony presented nothing that seemed out of the ordinary and none of the people there knew about Mr. Facsimile. Growing desperate, I recoup my thoughts and ponder about my next course of action."It seems that our person of interest is nowhere to be seen.

I think it is safe to assume that must have been where Facsimile stayed for the night. And with no one knowing where he is, then that means...""Is everything alright?"A sudden voice came behind me."Eep!""Did I scare you? I'm so sorry. It's just I saw you all and about looking at our staying rooms, so I thought it must have been because you are interested in renting a room for the night.""A-ah! Thank you for the kind offer, but I was just looking for a... friend of mine. I was told that he was staying in a room here in the pub, but I cannot, for the life of me, seem to find him."

"Is that so? Well, I feel that your search shall prove fruitless then. If your friend indeed stayed with us, then I could imagine he has already left by now.""I figured as much. Is there a way I might know where he went?""Unfortunately, I'm just a simple housekeeper, so your guess is as good as mine. If you have any question, you can always go to the front desk and ask Suzy. She keeps in check what comes out and what comes in, so you'll have more luck there."

"I appreciate the suggestion. Thank-"At that moment something caught my attention, a small crimson like stain on the corner frame of the door next to her. I had come to this door earlier when I spotted the battered clock, but I had not stopped to inspect the actual frame of it. It looked to be already dry, but I was certain that it must be blood.

//Barely visible, but judging by the dryness of it suggests it must have been some time ago. If Facsimile did in fact leave not too long ago, then that must mean that this was before he left. The question is, though, why is there blood there? Peculiar, I should take a picture and let Mr. Allegro know about this.//

"Is something off?" she inquired.I reacted, remembering that I was not alone."Hm? Ah, Apologies! I spaced out there for a moment. I was simply, um, admiring the structural design.""Of the doors?" she asked, puzzled."Y-yeah. I have a friend of mine who's studying interior design, so it just reminded me of him. Do you mind if I take a picture of this corridor?""Um, sure.""Much appreciated. There, perfect. Sorry for the odd request, but I know he would have never stopped bugging me if he did not have reference regarding shiren architectural work."

"It's alright. I'm well aware how friends can be sometimes when it comes to favors." "Agreed. But, in any case, thank you for all you have done for me. I hope you have a good day.""Of course! We're always here to help at Ol' Ale. Hope to see you again soon."Approaching the stairs, I tried communicating with Mr. Allegro, for he has not given me a single during my time investigating the floors. It was in vain, however, for I was not getting any sound of him. Growing worried, I descended the stairs quickly to find out if something was wrong. I finally understood why I was not getting replies.I was greeted by a hideous scene.

The once merry mood I was introduced with turned animalistic, as the jolly patrons were left screaming and yelling curse words at what was unfolding. A confrontation was taking form between my companion and two drunk, burly gentlemen. He was drinking on the table, not paying mind to the surrounding chaos."Is that Mr. Allegro? What is he doing?!"Suddenly, the man with the black vest picked my friend by the collar and looked down upon him."I must be imagining things. Can you run that by me again, boy?" he said in anger.

Mr. Allegro was looking at them in annoyance, not paying mind to the height and state of his opponents. Although he appeared to display a sort of poker face, it became noticeable that by his choice of words, he was clearly enjoying this."Heh, if your stupidity blocks your hearing capabilities, then allow me to repeat myself: If you got time to drink, then

I'm sure you have the time to be quiet. You see, I'm looking for someone right now at the pub and you are making this search rather difficult. Not to mention you've ruined the enjoyment of my drink. What an embarrassment! I expected more from a captain of the Bogshire military fleet!"

"Why you little!""Tch, small fries still got a mouth, does he? Looks like we're gonna have to beat this pipsqueak into shape and teach him some manners!"A sudden flush of air was rippling on the air when suddenly my friend managed to deflect the blow to the side. The shock left both men surprised, with a kick following up as it resonated towards his neck, knocking him up flat on the nearby table set."Fred! That's it! You're dead!"Pulling a knife from his back pocket, he came rushing down towards my friend.

As he noticed the brute being armed, he positioned himself into a stance and readied for the lunge. Close enough, he grabbed his dominant hand, tweaked it, released the knife and swept him off his feet, falling upon impact.The patrons were astonished by the outcome. They were whispering how he had beaten both those regulars without even a sweat despite having a height disadvantage. With the tables broken down and all the utensils on the floor, it was all a complete mess."Come now, what ever happened to civilities? And here I thought they would put more of a fight. Hm? Oh Hawkins! Good to see you again. Did you have any luck?"

"Ha-ha, oh you know..."Approaching him, I pulled him to whisper him anxiously."What happened? I thought we agreed to keep a low profile!""That was the idea, yes, but as you are keenly aware, I was met with two drunken sailors.

I wanted to take advantage of that to further our investigation, but unfortunately, they didn't want to cooperate.""S o, you decide to beat them into submission? What kind of quack plan is that?""It's not a 'quack' plan, it was a last resort plan.""Good Lord, you are insane. Wait, are you hurt? Here, let me call a doc-""Nonsense, I'm fine. I'll just clean myself up when we're done for the day. Did you get any findings on his whereabouts?"

As I was going to respond, I felt the pressure everyone directed at our directions with wide-open eyes in complete silence."He-he," I laughed sheepishly. "how about we go outside first?""Very well."Outside, next to the alley we continue where we left off."Now, what did you find?""Unfortunately, not much. I spoke with one of the housekeepers and she mentioned that all tenants that stayed in have already l eft.""Regrettable. Any other details that caught your interest?""Only two, the first one being a broken-down clock on one of the walls, marking 10:45. I took a picture of it in case you are curious, see for yourself. As for the other one, I noticed a strange crimson like stain on the frame of the door in front of it. It looked dry, but I am certain that it must be blood."

"Fascinating, and no one noticed that?""No, not even I would have noticed that if it was not in due to the conversation I had with the housekeeper. Since it is so minimal, it is hard to spot it unless you focus your attention on it.""I see. Then I'll message Gushi so she can dispatch someone from forensics right now. Anything else?""Oh! Actually, yes. I found this small button below the bed of that room as well. I think it might be some cuff button thanks in due part to the size. And when you consider that he was spotted staying here, I bet it is safe to conclude he was staying here.""How very apt of you! That certainly is a possibility. I'll be sure to look at it. Besides that, is there something else?"

"No, nothing. Like I said, she told us to check the front desk and speak with a lady called Suzy if we were looking for Mr. Facsimile.""Then what are we standing for? Let's ask her."Knowing the reputation he has built in the pub, I decided on an alternative."I... think it would be best if I ask her, considering the impression you left there.""What impression?"

//Get a clue please.//

"Hm?""Never mind.""So be it," he shrugged. "Just make sure to get to the point and not waste any more time than what we've done. I'll be on the cab if you need anything else."

//I am pretty sure you were the one wasting time by picking fights at a pub...//

My patience waning with my partner, I entered once more and greeted the beautiful, tanned woman behind the desk. She did not seem to be from around these part for her auburn hair was particularly different in contrast to all the women I have seen so far in this country."Hi there!" she greeted amicably. "Will you be renting a room with us?""Not today. I actually wanted to ask you a question.""Well shoot away! We're always happy to help around these parts. What can I do you for?""I have been looking for a friend for a while, but I have not seen him. He stayed in one of your rooms. I was told by the housekeeper that they already left, so I wanted to know around what time did he checked out."

"Oh! I see. Well, I can't exactly be telling you what time exactly he left since that information is strictly confidential regarding the privacy of our customers, but what I can tell you is that all of our tenants must check out before 11:00am. Any check out later than that is charged extra for the day."

//11:00. Hold on, the clock stopped working at 10:45. If that is the room he was staying in, might have something happened ten minutes before he left? And then there is the blood. Could it be his or someone else entirely?//

"May I ask where you saw him head?""I couldn't make heads or tails where he was going exactly, but he seemed in a hurry. I did see him walk with somebody, though.""He was with someone?" I asked, alarmed."Yeah!""And you are sure about that?""Yup! I might not look like it, but I always pay attention to people who come and go from the pub."" Then you must have gotten a glimpse of them, correct?""As embarrassing as it sounds, I couldn't. They had some sort of cloak on them, so I couldn't get a clear view. Oh, but they looked small and thin if that's something to go by! Other than that sorry hon," she said in embarrassment.

//Was he planning to skip the country? Surely you would not go away if you were not involved, right? And what of this second person? Could it be perhaps our fourth person Mr. Allegro was alluding to earlier? This plot just keeps thickening the more we keep diving. I have to report this to Mr. Allegro quick.//

"I understand. I appreciate your assistance nonetheles s."Remembering the disruption of Mr. Allegro, I decided to apologize to the lovely lady."Ah yes, I almost forgot.

My apologies for the confrontation between my friend and those hooligans earlier.""Oh that? Don't worry about that, dear. We're used to fights happening here, so it was just another day for us. Normally we intervene when the drunks roughhouse a bit, but it seemed that it kind of fixed itself on its own with that pretty boy earlier. Never seen a small jackal like him kick ass like he did, though.""I am inclined to agree," I said awkwardly. "In any case, I hope you have an excellent day.""You too! We hope to see you again in Ol' Ale!"

Chapter 8

3rd Moon

27th Phase

2018

3:55 pm

With the concerning news on my mind, I rushed with urgency towards my companion, deep in thought with all that's transpired today."Mr. Allegro!" I exclaimed." Hawkins, this better be good. I was in the middle of something-""Never you mind that for now, we have to go! Mr. Facsimile, he's not here and I believe he might be leaving the country!"He became alarmed at this unexpected development."What time, then, did he leave?""It must have been a few minutes before 11:00am. Policies state that all tenants must leave by that time in order to start preparing for further guests staying in the rooms.""I see. Did the front desk see where he went?""Regrettably no. She did, however, see someone with him when he left.""Really now?"

"Yes. They were cloaked, though, so she could not see anything beyond his figure.He rubbed his chin, pondering at this."Well! I think it's safe to say that something really is afoot! And that he is in need of questioning. Very well, it might be a long shot, but it might be our best bet."My partner picked up his telephone, marking the numbers to send a video call towards Ms. Okeanos."Come on, pickup," he uttered."Hey Luci! Hm? Oh, and Jenny! Hi-hi! What are you guys up to-""Skip the pleasantries, Okeanos. We're in a bind at the moment, and we need some assistance.""Of course, of course! It's always all job and no games with you, is it? Ha-ha! What can I do for you, then?""We need you to track our person of interest. We have reason to believe he might be skipping country. His name is Frederick Facsimile. I just sent you his phone number so I would appreciate it if you could track his phone."

"Huh?! You got his number?""You do know I'm not a hacker, right?""But you did learn something about it. I'm sure you still have that program on your computer you made with Quixote.""Fair point! Just give me a minute.""Ms. Okeanos, you too?!""How on Terra did you get his phone number?"I took a note of the logbook earlier when the front desk was unoccupied. It was before I spoke with the large brutes. I wasn't planning to use it since I surmised we would find him at the pub. But it's not like we have much of a choice to use it now, is there?""But is that not illegal?" I asked, concerned."It's not illegal unless you get caught.""You did not just say that, sir."

"Done! I sent you the cords to your phone, Luci!""As helpful as always, Okeanos, thank you."Sighing, I resign knowing that it would prove fruitless trying to change their mind."I cannot say I approve of this but, there is not much we can do. So, thank you.""Of course! Happy to help! Good luck!"With a smile and a wave, Mr. Allegro hanged up the call."Heh, starting to regret working with us now, rook?""I fear that what we are doing is a bit too much and might get in trouble because of it.""Nonsense! So long as we catch our witness, we'll be fine. That's the benefit of working as a private company with the authorization of the cabinet! Besides, this is relatively tamed in comparison to my other excursions."

//Tamed?!//

"Ha-ha, I'm joking. At least the last part."

//Our witness might leave country and he is making jokes?!//

"Anyway, it would seem that he's on Edinburgh Station. I deduce that with a few shortcuts and a few red lights, we might be able to shave thirty minutes and make it barely. Let's make haste. Raoul, full speed! The chase is on!""Ha-ha with such fire in your eyes, who am I to not say no!""Ah, Raoul slow down!"We hurriedly made our way towards the traffic, bobbing and weaving the incoming vehicles, taking shortcuts from places I was not even aware that existed. Finally, with the chauffeur landing on the entrance of the station, we exited and ran as fast as we could so that we would reach him before the train departed. With not a second to spare, Mr. Allegro bought the tickets with speed and precision, barely making it in time to reach the train before the doors closed for us.

"Hah, we managed somehow," I said as I tried to catch my breath."Somehow is correct, I did not expect for this to turn into a marathon. It's a good thing your hunch was right, Hawkins, for I believe all would've been lost if we were just a second too late. Speak of the devil... and he shall arrive."On the end of the cart, by the side of one of the booths, a man matched the description we had been given of Facsimile. He was a scrawny, round shouldered man who exhibited a singular olive vest with a black dress shirt, toppled with a cravat. He wore a monocle on his left eye, for he appeared to be partly blind. His hair was wavy, but it was kept in an organized manner."Well, thanks to the stars, we found him."

I spoke."Agreed. Come, let us cross-examine him before he notices us."Drinking coffee with a book to the side, he took notice of my companion and I."Would you mind if we sit here sir?" asked my companion amicably."But of course not. Please."He gave a gesture of invitation, which in return we took."Well, you look positively drenched and beaten about. Late for the afternoon trip, eh? Ah, well, I can't blame you. It usually gets packed at this time of day." He remarked in amusement."Yeah, well, you know what they say, 'Never any space, never any time'. If it wasn't because our driver knew the fastest route to arrive at the station, my friend and I would've missed the train.

"Facsimile chuckled at his remark."Well, you wouldn't be the first. That's how things usually go. Everything suddenly becomes harsher whenever you're in a hurry. That is why

I rather plan things that leave it at the last second.""I am inclined to agree. Hm? Caramel mocacchino I take it?""Why yes, it is. I take it you must be a fellow coffee aficionado?" he asked, impressed."Heh can't live without it. Especially when the beans are toasted just right."Enjoying their interactions, he chuckles at my companion, to which the attendant came to us."Good afternoon! Would you care for something to drink?"

"You certainly are turning to be an interesting fellow. Could I get you something?""The same you're having. I'm feeling for some coffee as well. Hawkins?""O-oh, um, some water is fine.""Of course. Would you care for something as well, sir?" "Hm? No, no, I'm fine at the moment.""Understood. I'll be right back."Leaving to fetch the beverages, we continue where we left off. "So where did you say you were from? He asked curiously."Victoria. Raised in the Queen's Kingdom."" Interesting! Returning home, then I take it?""Of course. Love here and I got engaged, so we just want to bring the news to the family."

//E-E-Engaged?!//

Growing red faced, I look away in embarrassment."He h, how charming? Well, you certainly caught a beautiful girl. Lucky you.""Ha-ha, yes well, I'm just grateful she chose someone as me to be her husband. Definitely used a life's worth of luck.""Ha-ha, that is how it usually goes!" said Mr. Facsimile in enjoyment.//Ugh, I hate this so much, and I hate it that his acting is good.

//With the train attendant returning to us, she gave both my drink and his.//

Taking advantage of the opportunity, Mr. Allegro and I drank our refreshments as the train whisked us away through the outer fields of Edinburgh."Thank you for the refreshment. Nothing really beats good coffee after a day of work. Now, with all these questions, I suppose it's fair I get a chance to ask something?""By all means! You've certainly proved to be a charming pair, so I'm all ears.""Excellent! Well then, tell me, what were you doing on the night of the murder?"Shocked at the question, he spilled his drink on the table."What on earth do you mean?" he said warily."Let's not do this, please. I really don't enjoy cliches and I'm not a fan of the back-and-forth banter you typically see in dramas. Come on, what other reason would we be sprinting to reach the last train of the day? We would appreciate if you cooperated with us. After all, running away from the law is a considerable offense, especially since we know you're involved in this ordeal."

"Hah, so much for a friendly pair. You two must be officers, then?""No, we're not," my companion quickly rebuked. "I would be caught dead, becoming one of those lapdogs. No, we're private investigators. My name is Allegro and my companion here is Hawkins. We're investigating the killing of Victor Primo.""Well," he snickered. "I believe that you are wasting your time, then. I have nothing to do with the killing. That much is true.""Is that so? Then tell me exactly why are you on a train to Victoria then? Surely, if you are innocent, you would have given the officers your account before you left."As I observed, our acquaintance had gotten quiet at the questions, still maintaining a smile to the side. Unfazed, he gave his response."As much as I would like to continue this little game with you, I have no reason to answer you.

If you two are not police officers, and for that matter, working with them, I will remain silent. If that is all you came here to do, then please exit at the next stop. You're making unnecessary attention towards us."My friend, as I had observed, was growing impatient. He sought to make this as smoothly as possible, but it was going against his favor."Why must people always make things complicated? Very well, if that is how you want things to play out, then so be it."With a few buttons pressed, it looked like my companion had sent a message."If you plan to make this harder, then I have no choice but to involve the officers.

I had every intention of speaking privately with you, but that bridge has been cut."His smile twitching. It had proven that this unexpected development had gotten through hi m."What happened to not being involved with the police?" he said, outraged."We aren't, but we are working together, so there's that. I ask that you just sit down and wait until we arrive at the next station, unless you plan on jumping the train, that is. Oh and thanks for the coffee," he said with an arrogant smile.His composure returning, he laughed off the sarcastic remark."Cheeky brat. You planned this from the start.""Did I?"

"Don't mock me!"In anger, the man threw a punch at my companion, to which he quickly grabbed by his forearm and threw him towards the floor, bouncing with the utmost pain from the impact. With the sound, everyone caught attention to the situation and starting murmuring about what had happened."That should prove an end to that. And our stop is here, wonderful! Hawkins, do me a favor and apprehend him. The officers should be waiting for our arrival at the station, so it would be best if we gave them Facsimile, without any problems."With the sunset coloring the sky, we arrive at Dunchester Station. Clearing the way for our detained, we walked towards the meeting point and gave them Mr. Facsimile so that they would then take him to the detention center where he would be kept detained for when interrogations.

With our duties done for today, we sit on to catch our breath."So, I take it we are done, yes?" I asked."For today we are. I just messaged Raoul to come pick us up here in Dunchester. Should take no more than twenty minutes to arrive.""Wonderful. But still, dear, what an eventful day.""I agree. I'm more impressed though that you managed to handle today it rather well for it being your first day working for us. Well done.""O-oh thanks! This investigation came rather abrupt for me, but I am glad that I was able to help for today. I still have a long way to go, so I hope I can still keep learning from you."Sharing my feelings with him, he was caught off guard, not expecting that from me. And despite trying to hide it, he shared a smile at those sincere words.

"Flattery will get you know where, Hawkins. But so long as you continue to apply yourself, you'll start growing in this field.""R-right!""Hm, we should revise all that we have gathered to close for today. Hawkins, give me an account of everything that has transpired.""Right away, sir."Picking up my journal, I searched through my journal the notes I made in our investigation."Our victim is Victor Primo, the headmaster of the house of Primos. He was murdered last night with what seems to be a kitchen knife. With no alibi, Mr. Jeffrey Hoper is the prime suspect.""Right, that's how the crime scene looked like. What else?""A huge discussion was heard over the residency. The discussion was so loud that members of the staff could hear muffles throughout the house, although no clear words. As noted by Mr. McKenzie, the walls are made of some noise cancelling materials, making it possible to not hear completely what happened in the room."

"Which means anyone could have entered without anybody knowing. And because the bush and camera show that someone else had entered we can confirm that besides Facsimile an uninvited guest was present as well," surmised my companion."Correct. That is what I make of it so far as well. There's also the fact that as a consequence of the confrontation, some exchanges had been made, evidenced by the sorry state of the room.

We also learned that Mr. McKenzie was familiar with Mr. Facsimile. Although he shared some valuable information, it was evident that he was limited to what he could say, for we deduced that he is being blackmailed by Mr. Facsimile.""T o think he would blackmail someone to limit our findings. Dastard's more crooked than we thought.""I agree. And it does not help when he is also framing an innocent man.""Of course, there's also Mr. Hoper. While there is no alibi to disprove him as the prime suspect, his demeanor shows that he really is not involved in this. Which is more the reason to find the truth and clear his name. What other things did you write, Hawkins?"

"There is also the detail of the blood on the door frame, the small button and the clock at the pub. It was broken, but it was left marking at 10:45, presumably in the morning." "Indeed. We should expect results for tomorrow by Gushi's team first thing in the morning. Send me all of your notes and evidence via pictures so I can check it out. Here's my number. Send it through iBuddy.""Got it.""Mm, anyway, I think that's all we could do for today. We have a lot of work cut out for us tomorrow, so it would be best to call it a day."

"If I may ask, what exactly are going to be doing tomorrow?""Firstly, I believe we should pay a visit to Facsimile at the Detention Center. He should prove to be useful for the investigation, although extracting that information will be another matter to deal with. I also want to give another look at the murder weapon. I have a feeling that, with what we found today, we might achieve the truth about what really happened that night.""But for now,", he stretched himself briefly. "We should make way and eat something. Any cravings, Hawkins?""I appreciate the gesture, but I am not sure I should-"A sounding growl was audible between us.

//!!!//

I was growing bashful, for with all the excitement we had gone through on our journey, I had not eaten anything this afternoon. He gave a bewildered stare for which I was too embarrassed to look at. Laughing, for he did not expect to receive a resounding reply at the thought of eating out, he smiled."Now Hawkins there's no need to be shy. You haven't exactly eaten anything since breakfast, so there really is no need to hold back. Besides, you've helped me a lot today, so it's the least I can do."Despite first impressions, Mr. Allegro showed a very considerate side to his character. Perhaps he only grows cold when his attention is fully on work."Um, well... Are there any coffee shops nearby? I am not one to enjoy big meals, but I am happy as long as there is some coffee and sandwiches."

"Coffee?" he replied in shock. "Well, that makes this trip all the more worth it. I was also in the mood for some coffee. Let's head back to Edinburgh. There's a shop that an acquaintance of mine works at that serves excellent coffee. Other things such as baked goods, homemade sandwiches and even shiren cuisine are offered as well. Ah, our ride is here. Let's not waste time, Hawkins. You'll surely enjoy the drink when we get there."After a night indulging ourselves with the brilliant taste of coffee, we went our separate ways and planned to reconvene tomorrow morning.

Chapter 9

3rd Moon

27th Phase

2018

8:13 am

Barely waking up from my bed, my phone buzzed as my companion had sent me a message with instructions in meeting him at the Agency to discuss our next course of action. I longed to sleep in for the day, like how I used to do. The events of yesterday proved to be exhausting, and I was not ready to return from work. Between the fast-paced workflow and the constant meetings of new characters, it felt like a never-ending story just waiting to continue. However, because the case is far from over and there is much work to be done, I made the push to get off the bed and prepared myself.

Upon entering the Agency, I was greeted with Hypno on reception. In his own rude way, he mentioned that Mr. Allegro had gone to the roof and that he was expecting me.

So, without further delay I got on the elevator and followed his the instructions. And with just a few seconds I reach the top floor, the doors opening and exposing an unfamiliar scenery. The sound of two crested tits chirped in rhythm, as the sun rays penetrated throughout the foliage of the giant cherry tree, dancing with the symphony of the wind. It was a beautiful work of art. Placed near were various tables and seats, as well as various gardening tools that helped keep the lone tree alive.

"Oh, Hawkins, you made it," my companion greeted.

//You could say that...//

"Heh, tired I take it? Yeah, I know how hard it is for people to get used to the new work pace. Soon enough, you'll get used to it. Would you like some coffee? I made it just this morning with some of the beans I got from home."

"Is that a fact? And you do not mind?"

"Of course not. Please, enjoy yourself."

"Well, okay. Thank you in advance. Oh yeah, you seem to have recovered relatively well after the brawl yesterday."

"Naturally. It's more soreness than anything, really. It's nothing to worry about, though. Just another day of rest and I'm good to good."

"Well, that is good to hear. Just please try to take better care of yourself. I am not sure how the Agency would react to you getting injured. But good heavens, this coffee is marvelous!"

Upon contact, the acid of the cup played on my tongue, giving me that sensation I craved to wake me up while the aftermath was a bittersweet end that gave me the taste of satisfaction. The flavor was exquisite, for it had a very chocolate like taste, making the experience sweet and perfectly balanced with no actual need to add a sweetener.

"I'm glad you liked it," he smiled proudly.

"And you made this from scratch? That is remarkable!"

"Right? The beans are from a coffee bush I was given a few years ago after helping the Director solve an international case on Amani. The Director lacked the space to cultivate the trees, nor did he find the time to tend to it. So, he decided to give them to me instead. I was hesitant, but I ended up accepting the gift nonetheless. Since then, I've had quite the fascination for the science behind the drink. Whenever I'm not solving a case or filling reports, I usually prefer to study in my house with the hope of creating the perfect coffee blend."

His passion for the subject was showing, and I saw a new side of my companion. As I mentioned, my impression of him was that of a cold individual who would prefer to not chatter idly if it did not involve his interests in the cases he would be working. But between our short time investigating together and his passion for coffee has evidently shown me that he is more human than he prefers to show to others.

//I see. So that drink I saw yesterday was probably an experiment of his.//

"I was not aware that you had a passion for this kind of thing. Have you considered opening your own shop? Why, I believe you would have success if you share this with the people."

"I have. It's a goal I want to achieve in due time. But for now, those cards must be put on hold. I have pressing responsibilities that I cannot afford to aside. Between my job at the Agency and a few unfinished businesses I have yet to attend, I haven't had the time at the moment to work on it."

"I understand. Well, I hope I get to see the day when you finally reach your goal," I said earnestly.

"Heh, thanks. But for now, let's just enjoy this small moment."

After he spoke, we took a time to enjoy our cups of coffee. There was a moment of silence. Not because we had nothing to discuss. But because we were enjoying a quiet morning together, savoring the flavor and the aroma of this drink. It was pure bliss.

Once we had finished our drinks, he picked up both cups and placed them on the side of the table. With fascination in my eyes, I stare at him as he considered the elements of the coffee he had prepared for us.

"That was good but not good enough. Maybe if I adjust the grinder next time, it'll become a bit more bitter. I'll see what I can do when I get home. Hm? Oh, apologies for my rambling. Ahem, anyway, I normally make coffee for some of the members of the Agency, so if you ever want some, I'll be happy to serve you at my office."

"O-of course! Thank you."

He looked away, trying to not make contact, for he exhibited signs of being flustered. Still, I could see a hint in his face of a sort of smile appearing as he noticed how I enjoyed his company and the drink he had poured his heart on to. His jovial face soon changed, however, and I was once met again with his concentrated glare. His brow sunken, he picked up his balisong knife and started to play with it, trying to return to his normal composure.

"Returning to the matter at hand, I called you here to talk about our next course of action regarding Facsimile. As you remember, we left him at the hands of the officers at the detention center. This morning, they are going to be interrogating him and see what they can find. With all that we have shared with the officers, they should have a solid foundation on where to start. Seeing we can't meet with him right now, I decided to pass the time this morning by gathering information that we could use as leverage for when we meet him."

He placed a folder on a table filled with various documents I had not seen before.

"I had Hypno dig up some dirt on our Facsimile and it would seem he possesses ties to the Primo family beyond work. For you see, while Facsimile himself does seem positively wealthy, his family history seems to suggest otherwise."

"His family history?" I asked.

"Indeed. It would seem that the way the family earned their paycheck was not in any shape or form noble. Let's start with Facsimile. In 1915, his family was dealing with economic struggles. Food was scarce, inflation was happening, and the family of six was proving to be difficult to maintain. So, what did they do? Well, they applied for a loan. And to who? Nothing more than the Cugini family."

"Cugini family? That doesn't sound too familiar to me."

"It's not a common last name, more so when it comes from a dead language. But if you translate the name to English, you get Primo.

"You are kidding!" I reply, surprised.

"I'm afraid not. The House of Primo is just a variation name of the Cugini Family."

//So it's not a coincidence! This means that they share a history beyond just employer and employee. Fascinating.//

"Going back to the history lesson, after negotiating the deal was set, and the loan was addressed a total of one thousand deidras."

"One thousand deidras? Well, that seems hardly enough, if you ask me. I am sure you could make that in less than a month."

"Yes, you could, but you have to remember, my dear Hawkins, that inflation changed the worth of the economy of the country. What you earn now could earn you more than a warm meal and some lodgings for the winter in that era. Since 1915, the value has increased to 2794.0%. So, if the loan was a thousand deidras before..."

//Ah!//

"Then that would make it 20,000 alone!"

"Hm, not an easy loan to repay in a month now, is it? We haven't even taken note of the interests included nor the deadline. However, one thing is certain: While our victim was indeed a very kind gentleman, the family itself was not. And the effects of such debt are still present today. I asked for Hypno to dig some more information relating to that and we found that to this day his family is still suffering the consequences."

"That is horrible. No one deserves to suffer like that. I get that loans sometimes are sometimes needed, but to end like that? Unforgivable," I said with disgust in my voice.

With his silence, it is clear that he is also moved by pity for the victims, and the abuse that people with power and fortune do to the lesser ones.

"That is unfortunately the world we live in. And when money's not even a question, you can get away with anything. That's regrettably the truth. We can only correct it as best we can by shining a light towards the people. Which is what we're doing here, so that Hoper doesn't also suffer at the expense of the real criminal."

//The truth huh.//

"I made a copy of these files, so these are yours to keep. Make sure to review them by the time we interrogate him."

"Understood, will do."

"I cannot help but feel that this runs deeper, Hawkins. This proves to be an interesting case. A suspect who is clearly not the killer and a witness who shows signs of interest. I have an inkling of something, but I need to ponder all of this beforehand first."

I made note of this information from the history between the families and the debt, as well as the itinerary for the day.

"Oh! I almost forgot to ask!" I exclaimed. "Why are we at the rooftop exactly? Were we not to reconvene in the Director's office?"

"We were. And while you did give me a favorable first impression on your first day, it has become clear that we do need you to complete your onboarding process."

"But did you not say that would take place after we were done?"

"I did and I would prefer it but, after seeing the whole spectacle, Gushi and his men put you through yesterday, I think it would be best if you did it before we continue. Unofficially, you are recognized as a member. Systematically, however, you are not. Because you haven't gone through the guidelines and rules, you're not registered on the database. You haven't received your official Guardian unit nor have received a guardian weapon. Things like those are facilitated typically to our investigators to, not only help them settle in with all the tools at your disposal but also establish your identity as a private investigator and a member of the Agency."

//I suppose there was no way around it then. Although, I am more curious about this guardian unit he speaks of. What might that be?//

He gave a sigh at his words.

"I hate rules as much as the next guy, but unfortunately there are some we have to work on, so right now that should take priority."

"But what of the case, then?"

"It'll be on hold. I informed Gushi of this setback so we're going to meet with her in the afternoon. As for you, the onboarding process shouldn't take more than three hours."

"Three hours!" I exclaimed.

"Inside voice please."

"S-sorry..." I said, flustered.

He gave an audible sigh.

"Look, if you're worried that the trail will grow cold, then don't. Right now, we've made steady progress and the officers are going to let us know if they find out anything in their interrogation session. If you follow the instructions and work diligently, then I'm sure you'll be done before 12:00pm. In the meantime, you'll excuse me as I consider something at my office Ring for me if something is amiss. Goodbye and good luck."

And with that, he disappeared into one of the lifts. Knowing what I had to do, I decided to half-heartedly pick myself up and make my way to the Research and Development floor.

Arriving in the basement, I was met with the doors that lead to the department. With a sign illuminating the entrance, I was introduced to an unfamiliar sight, a discovery into a new world only a select few knew about. It was a very spacious white room that extended itself more than how it initially seemed. From work benches and instruments of science, to desks filled with people working on their computers, the constant buzzing was too great. Powered by solar energy and a few generators, the room was divided between two sections: the researchers and developers. Constantly investigating, the researchers are a team that focuses on finding solutions for everyday problems, with their target being to help the agents that work in the field. The developers, in turn, use the information they obtain, and, following the blueprints they received, start designing the tools and gadgets, going though multiple phases build and destruction until they finally get it right. The staff seemed to be around a hundred people or so, with four of them being team leaders, each with their respective unit. Simply by looking at their attire would display that they were a class apart.

Waiting, I decided to look around until Okeanos was done with work, perusing the floor in my own curious way. Within a few minutes, I was finally greeted by the mischievous engineer.

"Hey-hey!" she greeted warmly.

"Okeanos, it is good to see you again. How have you been?"

"With full energy! Luci gave me some coffee early this morning and I'm all fueled up! Ah, he does his coffee so good! I can just live with just drinking his stuff!"

"I have to agree. His coffee was great, and he said it wasn't his best."

"That's Luci for you. He'll always try to make anything it as perfect as possible. But that just goes to show you how passionate he can get with anything he puts his mind into. Are you getting used to our facilities? It's kind of big, but once you keep navigating, you'll know your Xs and Os."

"To be frank, it can feel like a maze sometimes. But, thanks to the map Hypno and Ciarda gave me, it has been easier to find where I have to go."

"Oh, you met CiCi as well? Great! She might not look like it, but she's the Agency's top undercover agent. Her expert hearing and smelling capabilities have granted the Agency to solve some of the most intricate cases related to the underground. It's because of her we can easily get information on certain gang members, crack hot spots and taking down trafficking cases. Honestly! If it wasn't because of her, we wouldn't have had half the success we have. She's also super vocal, and she's not one to shy from a conversation so long you buy her a beer or two." She smiled devilishly.

//Yeah, I received that memo earlier. Still positively impressive how her resume stands despite how she acts. I'm even surprised there's an Undercover division to begin with.//

"It seems I have underestimated her then."

"Yeah, most people usually do. You should talk with her and get to know her when you get the chance, again, so long as you bring her the good stuff," she said enthusiastically.

"Why do you look excited for me wanting to give her alcohol?"

"In any case, we should go straight to business! Come, come!"

She immediately picked up a computer she had brought with her and booted it up. She then loaded several programs. It read: ONBOARDING.EXE, PERSONALITYSYNC.EXE and RU LESANDGUIDELINES.TXT. She pulled two chairs, one for me and one for her, inviting me to sit down with her to begin the process.

"As part of your onboarding, you have to complete each of these programs. You have a total of three hours to finish them, but I'm pretty sure you can definitely do it before two hours. Ill be completely honest with you, two third of the programs you have to complete are relatively slow and a pain. It's mostly your typical company's do's and don'ts, what to always keep in mind when investigating, insurance eligibility, hours working, blah blah blah that sorta stuff."

"What about the other third?" I asked.

"Ho-ho, that's where it gets fun. For now, though, just focus on the first two. After you finish the program, you will be presented by an exam, testing if you really did read through it all. The minimum passing grade is 80%. They're not particularly hard but do make notes in case you need them. After that, review the rules and guidelines attached to the program. Finally, just sign your full name with the e-pen next to the computer and send the results and signature to the Agency's database. Don't worry, it'll automatically ask you if you'd like to send it."

"You are not staying here with me?" I asked, disappointed.

"I wish I could stay, I really do. But I have my work cut out for me today. Between a few blueprints some of my friends need evaluating, and assisting Dr. DoQuixote on a device he's working on, I haven't got the time. Both duties should take me no more than two hours, so I think I'll be back by the time you finish to check up on you. That way we can do the last step and be done with everything, having set up your Guardian and all that."

"Mr. Allegro said something similar, something about a Guardian unit and a guardian weapon earlier. What exactly is a Guardian?"

"Hm, think of it..."

"Yeah?"

"Like a guardian."

"Brilliant," I replied with sarcasm.

She gave a sheepish shrug.

"Hey, don't blame me I'm just following orders! I'm not allowed to explain anything Guardian related to recruits until they finish the onboarding."

I gave a sigh, for my curiosity was piqued, but it could not be quenched. Knowing that this conversation was going nowhere, I decided to get started.

"Very well. I will start working on the process."

"Wonderful! If you ever need something, feel free to message me. For now, see ya!"

And with that, the scientist picks herself up from her chair and headed off to continue her work. With resolve, I began to work my way to complete the program swiftly, so that I may return to work with Allegro and continue where we left off.

After two PAINFULLY long hours, I was finally done.

"Ugh. Finally, I am done..."

I was exhausted by the constant reading. If that wasn't bad enough, the exam was even more extensive than the reading itself. It truly felt like there was no end. Suffice to say I was done with everything and finished the exam with a 90% score. In celebration, I fist pump into the air, satisfied that it was over. Despite the happiness I felt, I could not see where Okeanos was. She mentioned she would be done approximately by the time I was to finish here. Deciding to give my friend a ring to see where she was, she answers she answers and apologizes for being late, making her way towards me.

She was exhausted, for she came running with great haste, like her life was on the line.

"I'm... ugh, gimme a minute."

She collected her breath, apologizing in the process.

I'm so sorry! I was caught with all the work that I forgot you were doing this onboarding stuff!"

//It's been two hours! How the devil did you forget that in just two hours?//

She cleared her throat, trying to change the subject.

"A-anyway! You finished the program and attested you had read the guidelines. Good job! The only one left is the Personality Quiz."

She began entering her credentials on the program left opened and began giving her explanation.

"As you're aware, P.Is often have to undergo dangerous operations. More than anything, they get involved with criminals as petty as smalltime thugs to as big as crime lords. For that reason, thanks to our technology and the Agencys history, we were able to create the Guardian program.

You might be asking, what's a Guardian? Well, simply put, it's this little guy!"

"Hello!"

A sudden voice came about. It was originating from Okeanos' necklace.

"My name is Charlie! I am Guardian Unit#014. My host is Pelagic Okeanos and I am currently 4 years old! Pleasure to meet you!"

"Fascinating! An AI!" I cried.

"Yup! This here is my Guardian, Charlie."

"Hi, I'm Charlie!"

"Pff, she got it the first-time little guy."

Amazed at the technology, sparkles start to dance on the corner of my eye, impressed at the scientific feat this organization has achieved.

"Fascinating! I cannot believe that AI technology is real! I know that AI has been a rather known trope in fictional stories but I cannot believe that it's real!"

"Hehe, well, it's as real as it can get," she asserted proudly.

"But how? How does this Agency have this technological knowledge?"

"That's a secret!"

"Oh, come now!"

"He-he. The technology has been researched for more than forty years, but the actual product was came to be twenty years ago. I can't say much regarding the science behind it, but the founder of it is Dr. Juan DoQuixote, the Head Scientist of this department. He's not here now, but I'm sure you'll run into him, eventually."

//Dr. Quixote then. With something like this, he is surely a marvel of man. And if he has the knowledge and is possibly aware at the hurdle of the science community, why not share it with them?//

"Mhm! Charlie here is a second-generation unit. Errors are the tools we used to better everything for the CDA, so this little guy is here thanks to the earlier models. You might be curious on why Charlie is who he is instead of being your black and white AI. Well, it's because we program our AIs with a personality. We do it for the purpose of making the users feel more comfortable speaking with them, making them feel more like people than artificial intelligence. Don't worry though, the AIs aren't much of a chatterbox, so they'll only talk unless directed to them. As for the program here, it's a type of personality test. Based on what you answer, the program will build the best possible archetype that meshes with the personality you possess. You answer a few questions, mention a few preferences and voila! It's done! It's not complicated and once you're finished, all you have to do is download it to an usb and install it on your accessory of choice."

Accessory of choice?

"Yes, an accessory! The Guardian system is a symbiotic relationship. In order for them to actually function correctly, they need to create contact with their host because, well, they kinda, sorta take a bit of your vitality."

"I beg your pardon?"

"I can explain it to her!" interjected our small companion."

"H-hey!"

"Us Guardian units need nourishment to function! Like appliances, we need a power source so that all our functions work correctly as designed. Without it, we go to sleep, becoming useless to our hosts. That's where your vitality comes in! The scientists and engineers have developed a way to transfer energy from your body to us. On standby, we can operate on low energy consumption, performing basic task that can assist you. However, whenever you need to draw your weapon or other more complicated tasks, for the sake of maintaining our form, we create stress on our user's body so that we work as intended. As long as we can create contact with our host, we can absorb the energy and convert it as a form of battery."

"Hey, I was suppose to tell her that!"

"Sorry! I just got a bit excited!"

"Hmm. Pff, I can't exactly stay mad at you now can I? There's more to it than that, but we can discuss the other parts another time."

//Now I have seen everything. Symbiosis, weapons. What kind of Agency did I get myself involved with?//

"In any case, you shouldn't worry about screwing up the app. Ill be helping you out on this part so that everything goes smoothly. So, shall we begin?"

Okeanos started working her magic, and in matters of a second, we were greeted with an AI with a voice that resembled a woman.

"Greetings. If you have just booted this program, I would like to welcome you to work with us in designing your very own Guardian."

"Oh!"

"My name is Alexandra. I am Guardian Unit #001, and it is my upmost responsibility to explain everything there is to know about the Guardian program. The Guardians are a set of artificial intelligence designed to assist their hosts in their duties. We normally are entrusted to our fellow investigators, but some of the people of other departments are entrusted with a Guardian as well, depending on their activities. Some functions can extend from simply recording findings, scanning surroundings to conventional tools like mentioning the time or finding the temperature of the environment. However, that is not the only thing that we offer."

"As you have been keenly made aware, the Guardian program is a system that was designed to serve as a tool for our fellow investigators to undergo operations smoother when dealing with criminals. However, Guardians can serve also as a combat weapon. There are two modes that are included when on its weapon state. Lethal and non-Lethal. They are some key differences between both states. When used on Lethal mode, the weapon will take a more decisive approach. It significantly drains a lot of the energy of their users when on prolonged usage. Lethal Mode can only be used if you find yourself in a do or die situation, where your only option is to fight and claim their life. Non-Lethal mode, however, offers a more cautious approach. It is mainly used when dealing with criminals who are either unarmed, possess no visible threats, or if your objective is to incapacitate them. It drains less energy, however. While you do have these options available at your disposal, we encourage everyone to find a more peaceful solution. These weapons are designed to bring peace to the people and must only be used as a last resort."

"To make our units feel comfortable with the Guardians, this program serves as a genesis to what your Guardian will be designed to speak and act in accord with the choices you pick. It should not take less than an hour and it should be relatively simple.

Now for our disclaimers.

"Disclaimer: We are not made responsible for misuse of the Guardian systems. If you use your Guardian against civilians, you may be put on a position of being prosecuted by the law. By no means will we help you or represent you, for this is a responsibility you alone must carry. If we find traces of modifications in your Guardian unit, your privilege might be revoked, punished, or even expelled from the Agency. You are also not allowed to lend it to anyone that is not you. Failing to comply with the rules and terms of conditions will lead to immediate termination and possible charges based on the situation you are being accused of. Disclaimer done."

"If you have any additional questions, feel free to ask your overseer. If not, then please click the link on the corner right to begin the personality examination so that we may begin designing your very own unit. My name is Alexandra, and it has been a pleasure garnering your attention. Remember, there is no Guardian like your own Guardian."

The AI soon popped out of the screen, and we were greeted with the familiar display we had initially seen in the beginning.

"Well, there you have it! Alex explained it in detail, but just in case something came to mind, do you have any questions?"

"No, I think I am fine. I am starting to understand, but I admit that this makes the head spin around with the kind of technology I am dealing with. She mentioned she was #001. I take it she was the first unit created?"

"Yup! She was designed and created by our very own Dr. DoQuixote and an old friend of his. But that's a story for another time. Now let's continue, Ill be taking control here, so just give me your response for each of the questions I ask you."

Okeanos clicked on the button and the questions started. There were a total of 30 questions each divided into five sections: General, Likes, Dislikes, Preference and Goals.

We started to work on the questions diligently and, with Okeanos's assistance, we managed to finish in thirty minutes.

"And we're done! The AI should be done in a few seconds. Oh, never mind, it's done!"

After letting the system boot up and configure all that was necessary, a friendly voice came about.

"Greetings. I am a Guardian unit #58. I have been designed to work together with Investigator Hawkins and assist in all that I may."

"And there you have it!"

"Whoa."

"Ahh, I know I've done this for some time, but seeing another baby come into fruition with all the zeros and ones does make me smile. Give it a name, Jenny!"

"You do know that this is not a pet right," I replied, baffled.

"Oh, come on, don't be such a spoiled sport! In order to use the AI's capabilities to the fullest, you have to form a strong relationship with them. Trust is the first building block of a symbiotic relationship. Did you not hear the robot lady? You're going to be spending some time with it. That's essentially why I encourage everyone to start by giving them a name. So, stop nagging and give them a name!"

After persistently bugging me about the issue, I half-heartedly complied with her.

"Alright, fine, stop pulling me back and forth, will you!"

"Yay!"

"I swear. Anyway, let me see. I think I'll call you... John."

"Entering new naming parameters, please hold. Done. I am Guardian unit #58 and my name is John. It is a pleasure to make your acquaintance, Ms. Hawkins. I thank you for giving me life and I will do my best to assist you. As... soon as I am implemented in an accessory, that is."

"Aw, your Guardian is so polite. That's adorable. Now that we're done with that, we should to focus on the accessory you want the Guardian to be on. Tell me, do you have any preference?"

"What are some of the choices?"

She picked up a small box she had left off on a nearby table.

"We have from bracelets to watch to even earrings and necklace. Finger rings are also available, and we can even do some customizing on any of the options."

//This feels like more like a sales pitch than anything.//

"I have a necklace and Lucio has a ring."

"Oh, so that's what it was. I remember he speaking to it, so that must be it."

"Yup, so what'll be?"

I gave it some thought. Finally, I spoke my mind and gave my response.

"A watch is fine if it is alright with you."

"Super! Then I'll get started right away with my team. While I would have liked for you to take the Guardian with you, the chap is going to have to stay for a bit until I'm done. Don't worry, once everything is done, Ill personally give it to you on your investigation."

"I apologize. I just came to be, and already I have proven to not be useful."

"Aw, don't worry John, well get you set up so you can start working with Jenny and Lucio."

Knowing full well how earnest the AI sounded, I smiled.

"Yeah, don't worry, I want to return to the investigation as bad as you want so I'm sure Okeanos will get you set up in time during work."

"I... appreciate the sentiment. Very well. Until I am properly equipped, I wish the best of luck to you."

"I look forward to working with you, John."

"He-he. Well let's put you to sleep in the meantime okay little guy?"

"Of course. Initiating hibernation mode."

With a buzz, the artificial intelligence powers down.

"And with that I can start getting to work. Hm? If you're worried about him, he'll be fine. For me to install him he needs to be on a non-operative state I don't end up screwing up his system."

"I see."

"Yup! He'll be back up and running in no more than five hours."

"That's fast!"

"He-he, well when you're the second in command from R and D you can basically do anything!" she said proudly.

"I can see that. But still, thanks."

"Ah don't worry about it! Part of the job really!"

"Perhaps. But I still appreciate everything you have done for me. This workflow has proven to be rather fast for me, and despite my ineptitude to get used it you have been patience and kind to me for these past two days. And that means a lot to me."

Caught off-guard, she shares a stunned expression to me.

"Apologies if I made things awkward. I just have not had the time to express what I felt. Just forget I said anything-"

"No, you didn't make anything awkward! I just didn't expect for you to feel grateful. Besides Luci and Dr. DoQuixote, I don't get praise or acknowledgement very often. They mostly just think I do that out of obligation, so they don't bother. So, hearing someone just say thanks, as stupid as it sound made me a bit happy. But it's not like I want the praise. Just knowing I helped someone is enough for me. Besides, it's not like I deserve it to begin with."

"But everyone does deserve being praised though. It's what pushes to continue moving forward and keep doing what we do."

"You think so? I don't know. Sometimes I just feel like someone else could do my job. It's not like I'm unique or anything so why would someone like that deserve that kind of attention? "

Unable to respond. I respond in silence at those self-deprecating words. In truth, I did not expect this side of her.

From what I have gathered so far, she just seems like a bubbly and happy girl. But I guess everyone has their own demons they are fighting against.

//She really is just a sweet girl in the end. Although, I cannot help but feel bad she feels like that. Everyone has their own unique qualities. It is that uniqueness that makes living exciting, happy to meet new people that could bring spice on to your life. Because without spice, what is there to live in a monotone world?//

"Besides, a battery is needed to bring life to a machine. Without that battery, the machine dies," I said with a low tone."

"Hm? Did you say something?"

"No, I did not. Pay no mind."

"C'mon tell me!"

"What was I saying again?"

"I'm here pouring my heart to you, and you're hear speaking in a low tone tell me?! Now you're just being mean!" she said with a pout expression.

"He-he sorry. Do you know where Lucio is right now?"

"I don't know, do I?"

"You are such a child, you know that?"

Laughing, we take a moment to enjoy the banter, to which she then shares a smile, the attitude she is wont to show everyone.

"I mean it though. Never sell yourself short. And if you ever need someone to talk to, just know that I'll be here to hear you out."

"Jenny your accent slipped!"

"I-it did?" I express in embarrassment.

"I didn't know you could slip out from your victorian accent! That's crazy!"

"Please forget you heard that."

""Don't think I'll be able to! I thought you said you were victorian?"

"I am, but sometimes my accent goes away when I get emotional. Mother mentioned that Father was like that when I was young so I got him from him I guess. Ugh, I am ashamed of myself."

"He-he guess that must mean that your unicue quirk is that you can slip on and off your accent!"

Remarking with humor, she started to laugh loudly. Remembering my inquiry from earlier, she calms down to tell me.

"Heh, well Lucio's still up top. I think he's finishing up, so you should still be able to catch him inside his office."

"Will you be alright alone?"

"Of course! I'm extra motivated now so it's not like I'm gonna have time to start thinking of bad stuff! So go ahead, I'll call you when I'm done."

"Okay, good luck."

"You too, bye!"

Bidding her goodbye for now, I press onward to meet with my companion for the case, not wasting a second to continue our investigation.

Chapter 10

3rd Moon

27th Phase

2018

11:49 am

As I continued my walk, I was greeted by some fellow investigators on the second floor.

"Why hello there!" A red-haired, freckled man spoke.

"You must be the new blood that's been making sound throughout the building."

"Y-yes, I am. I was actually on my way to continue said investigation with Mr. him."

"Is that so? I'm surprised you haven't exactly quitted."

"Quitted?" I asked, perplexed.

"Yeah," his friend responded. Rumors have it that Allegro has never lasted with a partner because of his controversial personality. He can be tough on rookies, putting enormous amounts of pressure on them. I even heard that one of his old partners ended up being his lover. But because they got too close, work became a problem. Mix that with his more dominant personality and you got a recipe for disaster. She went and left fed up with him, taking her Guardian with her and not giving another word to him or the Agency."

"I see..."

"Yeah, mate. Not to mention he sometimes goes rogue, going above the rules by doing procedures that are not sanctioned or allowed by the Agency. Honestly, I'm not sure how the Director lets him get away with it."

"That's the golden boy for you," the lad in red shrugged. "When you're at the top, you can get away with anything."

This conversation was going foul, and I was not a fan of it. While I do understand that from what I have seen, Mr. Allegro can be a bit hard to work with. He still did not deserve this talk behind his back. I was beginning to grow visibly annoyed at this idle chatter."

"Not that it matters, but I would prefer if you would stop speaking rudely to Mr. Allegro. I was never one to enjoy speaking behind the back of someone. It shows a lack of etiquette and a lack of respect."

They both were left ill at my comments.

"Ay? I didn't know we had a teacher's pet with us. Can't even take a joke now, can you, eh?"

"Oi, be careful. Considering she's working with him; she might rat us out."

"She's not gonna rat us out. I'm sure she shares the same sentiments as us, besides you know how Allegro is. You think he's going to care?"

"Not particularly unless I catch said people speaking behind my back."

"Mr. Allegro!" we exclaimed unanimously.

"I-it's not what it looks like, mate!"

"Y-yeah! We were just speaking with the rookie to get to know her!"

"Oh? So besides speaking behind your co-workers, you were also slowing her down in doing her job, something you lot clearly have no idea how to do. Nothing to say? No? Then how about you turn in your reports on that assignment the Director gave you last week? Or else I'll make sure to note down how you two have been skipping on your duties and for the past week."

They left swiftly without a word, embarrassed by the sudden confrontation of their superior. Like a whimpering dog wagging their tails between their legs, they scurried. My companion here gave a deep sigh and tried his best to return to his usual composure.

"Slacking lot," he mentioned between his teeth. "Sorry about that, Hawkins. But even among our ranks, we have people would rather gossip than do their work."

"That is fine. Although..."

"Although?"

"I am more annoyed that people have the audacity to speak behind others like that. Especially when it is off some baseless rumor that is not even true. No one deserves that sort of treatment."

"I used to believe that some time ago. Now I'm not even sure..." he mumbled.

"What?"

"Nothing, don't mind me."

Dodging my question, he picked from his pocket some sort of card.

"Here, it's your identification. Okeanos sent me a message notifying me that you were done, so I quickly went to the print room and successfully managed to retrieve your card. Now, with all of that out of the way, I best think we should return to our investigations. A cab is waiting for us outside the lobby. Let us make our way towards our person of interest."

With Raoul behind the wheel, we drove towards our destination. Surprisingly, Mr. Allegro broke the silence with a conversation.

"So, how did everything go? Did it go swimmingly?"

"It went as best as I would hope for. I was intrigued, however, by the Guardian system and the AI programming."

"I would imagine. It's not something you see every day, nor is it something the public is even aware of."

He gave a glimpse of my direction and saw how I had no accessory attached to me.

"I see that you do not have your Guardian equipped, though. Is there a reason?"

"Oh, well, it is not done yet."

My companion cocked his head to the side.

"But I was informed you were done with everything. You did finish the whole process, yeah?"

"I did. However, Okeanos had not done the accessory for the Guardian. She told me to hurry up and reun te with you so that I am not to delay our investigation. She mentioned she would send it my way as we continued investigating."

"I see. Well, it's not like you could do anything. We should leave everything in her hands then. Off headed but reliable, that's the best way to describe. Now, onto pressing matters."

Out of his pockets, he pulled a few pieces of papers he had jotted down.

"While you were doing your onboarding with Okeanos, I decided to consider every detail we have obtained in my Mind Palace."

//Mind Palace huh? I think he said something about that yesterday as well.//

"You mentioned something along those lines yesterday when you were explaining the process of investigating. If I may ask what exactly a Mind Palace is?"

He grew in thought, finding the answer to my question.

"Think of it like this," he responded. "The Mind Palace is a technique I use on my investigations. It involves becoming familiar with your surroundings and giving a lasting impression on your head to achieve an answer. Your surroundings can include from places we have visited, the evidence we have collected and all the faces we have met. Essentially-"

"You transport yourself to the event in question based on all the evidence collected and try to find hidden clues that may not be physically there."

"R-right. That was quick of you to pick up."

"Fascinating, and you have used this technique ever since you started working with the Agency?"

"No, I've used this theory ever since I was capable of doing so. When I was small, some kids would ask me for help, be it for their lost toys or even finding their own parents. Naturally, I'd apply these principles and would solve their conundrums."

//Interesting. Who would have thought a child could put to practice such a technique?//

"Of course, this technique is not something most people can learn. It takes some time to master it, for you cannot afford distractions of anything. The simplest of things can break the virtual world and make you lose your progress."

"I think I understand now. It is the first time I have heard about this, but I am intrigued nonetheless. Is there a chance that I could develop this theory?"

"Obviously. It's not something that you cannot learn. As long as you apply the steps, it should come to you like your ABCs. Now, going back to where we left off this morning. While you were with Okeanos, I considered everything we had collected, and i found the answer that had no room for doubt."

After a brief pause, he let out a most startling revelation.

"Facsimile is involved in the killing."

I was shocked at the sudden accusation. We had in fact, found that he was present in the same room that day. That much is true. But to come to this conclusion with no evidence? I was left bewildered.

"Involved? Surely you do not mean to believe that he could have done it, do you?"

"Consider the facts Hawkins. We already know that he was indeed our third person, thanks to Hoper. He did all he could to silence his presence, from not leaving any noteworthy traces to him to even silencing some of the staff. In it is the truth, evidence such as Hoper's refusal to share any information pertaining to his identity and McKenzie's evasive character. Now, with Hoper's rebellious personality, you would think he would not clamp up regarding his presence. However, considering that Facsimile is a blackmailer, who knows what he told Hoper to keep his mouth shut. Same goes for McKenzie. If we hadn't offered our protection, he would never have given us a clue about his character."

"You do have a point there."

"As for the clock you mentioned yesterday, I decided to return to the pub and look for the blood stain. Luckily, it was still there, so I had my Guardian scan the blood and identify the owner's stain. And the owner ended up being McKenzie. So, why was the blood there? Because, a fight had broken up between both men. Facsimile had called him to discuss a way to leave the country, but McKenzie would not go with his plan. He tried to remind him of what would happen if he did not obey him but McKenzie stood his ground, until finally he came at him and attacked, breaking the clock in the process and leaving it in non-working conditions. This all happened in afterhours, which means that the 11:45 meant for the night and not the morning."

"Y-you must be kidding. How on Terra did you-"

"I spoke with McKenzie this morning and he told me about this as soon as I showed him the photos. Said he thought he had cleaned the blood before anyone noticed."

"But when did you have the time to do all this investigating, and when?"

"I couldn't get any sleep last night, so I just thought that I might as well continue working. So, I booked the room he stayed at the pub in the night and observed to my heart's content."

"I am impressed you discovered those facts in less than a day. But you should take better care of yourself."

"I'll be fine. As soon as we're done with this case, I'll get all the sleep I need."

"If you say so. Just try not to overdo it please. "

Hearing those words, his face grew pale suddenly.

"Mr. Allegro?"

"I-I'm fine."

//You do not look like it though...//

"Really, don't worry. Going back to what you were saying."

Sighing, I continue sharing my thoughts.

"Plain and simple, I can understand your line of thought. Suspicion arises from what we extracted from the pub and Mr. McKenzie's account, which would make Mr. Facsimile a possible suspect."

"Correct. Not to mention the lack of an alibi. The butler and maid both had alibis. I went ahead early this morning to confirm the alibis of the housekeeper as well, and they also presented no contradictions. The only person as of right now who hasn't given an alibi other than Hoper is in fact

Facsimile. Just as much as Hoper is considered a suspect, I believe that Facsimile should be considered a suspect as well."

In theory, what he exposed could explain every single detail we have observed of the case and put into another perspective how the crime occurred.

"Your theory seems to present an interesting angle," I said.

"But?"

"He presents no motive that I can remember now."

"Don't tell me you forgot already what we discovered yesterday? The history between Facsimiles family and the Primos? The history is the motive. Hawkins, it is my principle to believe that coincidences don't exist. Can you refute the fact that the descendant of that family who owed so much money was working closely with the late headmaster? Did the headmaster knew what injustice they had done to the family of the man and hired him so he could pay what was left of the debt? I do not have the answer to that. However, it doesn't change the fact that vengeance could be a possible motive."

"And what of the murder weapon? Do not misunderstand, I want desperately for Hoper to be freed of this wrongful accusation. But right now we haven't found anything that could suggest another way the victim could have died, let alone Mr. Facsimile."

He was growing visibly annoyed.

"Tell me, do you believe Hoper is the killer?"

"N-no but-"

"Do you have any other person of interest?"

"Not that I am aware of-"

"So, suicide?"

I was growing impatient at his contemptuous attitude.

"I understand where we stand at the moment, but we cannot just point accusations right now. It is too rash. Look, I am not dismissing your theory, for it fits every possible evidence we have right now. But before we jump to conclusion, I believe it is prudent to first meet with the person and hear his account."

At my words, he drew breath in an exasperated fashion. He relaxed his shoulders and found there was no point in discussing this any further. The day turned to be a very murky afternoon. Pouring in with gusts of wind, all we could see was nothing but blurs and the scatters of rains. Not a single soul could be seen out and about in this terrible weather. Only the sound that could be heard was the thuds of the constant raindrops falling onto the vehicle's roof and our collective breath. In less than ten minutes, the looming Detention Center was becoming apparent, for the fog was as thick as it could get on this boggy country. Not as harsh as Victoria, but thick, nonetheless.

"Hawkins," he interjected.

"Yes?"

"If you could not share what we have discussed on this ride with Gushiken, I would appreciate it greatly. Like I've already told you, she believes that evidence is absolute and unless we can prove that it did in fact take place as I have deducted, she won't hear any of it. There's an umbrella below the driver's seat. Make sure to take it and let's head out."

We exited the vehicle and pressed on. We were introduced with two angular great doors. The floor was dirty, filled with dirty and mud, made possible thanks to constant downpour and the soil fellow officers left behind upon entering.

"So, are we going to proceed with his interview?"

"No, not yet. Gushiken's still with him. We should reconvene with Hoper again and share what we have found out so far to see if he might illuminate anything new with our findings."

Chapter 11

3rd Moon

27th Phase

2018

12:25 pm

As we entered the lobby, Mr. Allegro and I were greeted by the familiar officers, Michael and Charles. Taking his time, my companion explained the purpose of our visit and, after a ring towards the captain, allowed us to follow with our questioning so long as we followed the same rule.

"Good afternoon, Hoper. I trust these officers have been treating you well," greeted my companion with interest.

With glad in his expression, Mr. Hoper stood up from his chair and approached the bars.

"Mr. Allegro! Ms. Hawkins! Oh, it's good to see you again! I want nothing more than my freedom, but I will admit that it caught me by surprise how kind they have been towards me."

"They might act rough, but for the most part, the shiren law is one that is just. Until the court recognizes your offense, and everything is proven definite, all officers must treat their prisoners with courtesy and respect."

"Well, I appreciate it, for I still feel disturbed for all that has transpired in the last days. In all my years as a lawyer, I have never dealt with a case relating to a crime. Having said that though, I suppose you did not come here for small talk now, have you?"

I pulled my notes from my messenger bag with the attempt to share our findings.

"We wanted to ask for your opinion in regard to some information."

"Of course! What can I do to help?"

"What do you make of McKenzie?"

"Mr. McKenzie? Well, he can be a bit of an oddball sometimes, but he's a very jovial man and an excellent teacher. He taught me everything there is to know when it comes to cooking. If I am to be honest, I felt he was not fond of me when I first came in. But be it for whatever reason. He grew attached to me in due time. Said something of reminding him of the days of his youth."

"Any rivals, enemies?"

"Not that I recall, no. Everyone always loved his company. Why are you asking me about him, though?"

"Blackmailing, Hoper," he said bluntly. "We have reason to believe that he was blackmailed by Facsmile."

"Blackmail? Preposterous," he scoffed. "Facsimile might be a snake, but I don't think he's capable of doing such a thing."

"Well, he is. McKenzie's choice of words, his silence and how he chose to withhold information seem to point to a interesting conclusion."

"And that is?"

"Isn't it obvious? For the murder of Victor Primo."

Realizing what my companion was getting at, he understood the conclusion.

"I see. So, you believe he must have done the killing."

As silence filled the room, my companion offered him a drink he had prepared in his spare time.

"Drink up Mr. Hoper, for I sense this might grow to be too much for you. It is too premature to say, for we have not spoken fully with him, but we do think he is involved."

"We caught him fleeing cross country," I noted. "Between the sudden death of the headmaster, the blackmailing and fleeing the law, everything points suspicion unto him."

"You jest. He tried to flee?"

"Yes. It was after we had finished conversing with you, we paid a visit to where he was staying at. It was then we knew he left and made haste to catch up to him, which, to our luck, managed to be. He is being interrogated right now by the captain, and we are to follow sooth with our own questions."

"Even so, I cannot imagine him killing anybody."

My companion raised an eyebrow as he drank.

"Why not?"

"Well, because of the nature of the crime. My friend's death was brutal, as you recalled. If he ever considered such a horrid deed, he would most certainly find a way to not draw suspicion. He is a very methodical man, you see, and he prefers to take the most practical choice in everything he does. Knowing him, he would just hire someone else to do the killing, creating an alibi in the process."

"Hm! I'll make note of that then. Ah yes, we have reason to believe someone else was involved in the night of the crime as well. Hawkins if you could."

"Someone else? Surely this is getting out of hand, don't you think?" remarked jokingly.

"No, we are not. Some evidence outside the house suggests that someone had entered the room through the window. How they reached the window is beyond us, but thanks to your testimony and that of Mr. McKenzie's regarding the camera yesterday, we can confirm there was an intruder present."

Growing astonished at what we had gathered on what little time we had, he rejoiced.

"Brilliant! To think someone else had entered the room. Surely that is enough to prove that I am innocent then!"

"It's still too early for that," my companion remarked. "We have no evidence that directly links us to the killer other than the knife you had with yourself."

"B-but! This does help our case in proving that someone else could have done it and pinned the crime on you, Mr. Hoper."

"I do not care; you have done so much progress and I am already indebted to you. I still do not think Facsimile could have done it, but I am sure you will find the truth by the end of it."

Seeing Mr. Hoper grow in high spirit at this revelation made me unconsciously smile. Despite our relatively fast pace, we have done so much since I started working on the case. And knowing that there is a chance we could save the life of someone made me happy.

"In any case, that is all we had to share with you. I thank you for giving us insight with Facsimile. From the look of the time, I think the officers might have finished interrogating your co-worker. If you'll excuse us."

Standing from his chair, he looked back towards the accused and reassured Mr. Hoper.

"If you truly are innocent, then the light will show it to everyone. Until then, keep your hope up."

"R-right! Thank you!"

With that we excused ourselves and exited towards the main lobby, where a fellow officer told us the captain was done interrogating Mr. Facsimile. Escorting us, they showed us the way where Ms. Gushiken was occupying herself.

She had just finished interrogating our person of interest. However, her expression was not at all inviting. Her brow was submerged, her eyes were darting, and her lips were quivering in anger. With her hands buried in her jacket, she grew frustrated with what I assume to be our Mr. Facsimile. Trying to control her temper, she was touching her right earlobe, where a lone star shaped earring stood shining.

"Still using that to control yourself, eh, Gushi?" said my companion in a dry, sardonic attitude.

At the sudden voice, she became flushed, growing rosy, red cheeks on her sides.

"LUCIO HOW MANY TIMES DO I HAVE TO TELL YOU TO STOP SNEAKING UP ON ME?!"

"As many times as I can keep getting you," he shrugged with a smug smile crossing his face.

//Mr. Allegro!//

"Why you little!"

Despite his fast reflexes, she still managed to grab his collar and showed signs of readying to come at him. He, in return, was smiling in a superior manner.

I was growing in anxiety. We had just arrived, and they were already going at each other, something we least needed right now.

"I am so sorry for the comments my companion made, Ms. Gushiken. W-we were just caught off guard by how you had portrayed yourself. Is everything alright?"

Carefully choosing my words, -for I less than desired to escalate the situation more than it was- I calmed her down. At least sufficiently enough to make her let go of Mr. Allegro, albeit in a rough manner.

"You're lucky your friend here is polite and nice enough to apologize to you. No, everything is not alright. The weasel's lips are sealed tight. He doesn't want to comply with us."

"Has he given a reason?"

"No, not at all, and that's just it! He didn't even let us ask him a few simple questions like 'How close were you with the victim?' or 'Do you believe anyone to be a suspect?' He just came and asked for a lawyer without a second thought. Normally when people don't want to talk, it's either because of fear or because he's protecting someone. Sure, he's being charged with evading the law but we have no intention of pointing at him for no evidence connects him to the crime. He just won't cooperate! Between this, no fresh evidence besides your lots of findings yesterday. We have nothing to go by. We're stuck!"

"Nothing new," murmured my companion.

//Can you stop trying to cause any more fights please?//

"Is there a chance we could speak with him, Gushiken?" I asked.

"You're welcomed to try, but I honestly think he has no intention of spilling anything."

"Well, we'll see about that. Come, Hawkins, let us meet our esteemed guest."

With a police escort, we reconvene once again with the gentleman with the smile, Frederick Facsimile.

"It is a pleasure to meet you, Facsimile. Our run in the train was rather quick, so whatever we discussed was rather limited. I've heard good things about you," expressed Mr. Allegro in a amicable tone.

"Oh? Have you? And what is it that you have heard?" questioned the gentleman with a smile.

"Well, the fact you have dedicated your life to working under Victor Primo, or rather, worked until he died. Such dedication is dully noted to be praised."

"Praises are not to be given. I was just doing my job, as everyone should do, although," he chuckled, "considering you people stand stuck in the investigation, I am not so sure you can call it that."

My companion gave a very audible chuckle.

"I can agree with you about that. That's the reason why they have asked me and my companion to help solve the case."

"I fear that you have wasted your time then. I mentioned earlier to those vulgar police officers that I was not going to speak until I had my lawyer besides me."

//A sudden chill came about from the other room.//

My companion, however, was good humored by his approach.

"Why is it then you need a lawyer? We personally don't believe you have an involvement with the crime. However, considering you used to work for the victim, we just want to ask a few simple questions about the lead suspect, Jeffrey Hoper."

"Is that so?"

"Indeed. The officers have their own point of interest, but we have our own. Fairly simple questions, really."

The gentleman in green raised a few eyebrows, questioning the words of my companion, but Mr. Allegros' poker-faced smile made sure to convince him that he was going to keep his word.

"If I am to be frank," he finally said, "I don't necessarily trust you, especially after the charade you pulled yesterday. However, considering you have been a very intriguing individual, I could do you the favor in answering these 'simple questions' you have. Don't expect me to answer them all, though."

"Rightfully so, and I thank you for your cooperation. Now, the first question is simple: in the house, how was Hoper usually like? Did he show any signs of having any aggression towards the headmaster?"

"Not that I recall, no. He was always a timid young man so I couldn't image that happening. A bit of a coward, if I may add, but he always did his job, and that won the respect and attention of the headmaster. You can imagine I was caught off guard when I heard the chap did the deed."

"So you believe he did the killing?"

"Who Mr. Hoper? It hurts, but I think so. Between the discussion and the fight the late headmaster and Hoper had, I would not be surprised it ended like that. Whatever they were discussing must have been something important to have caused this ending."

The talk continued for a few minutes, making a few notes here and there, although, if I am to be frank, I lacked the understanding of why he was asking these types of questions. My attention had gone awry, however, when I noticed something singular. Underneath the gentleman's fingernails, some white dried substance could be seen. It was barely visible, but I was sure that detail was present.

"Well, I think that's all the time we have for today. I thank you for your assistance, Mr. Facsimile."

"But of course, while I do not intend to involve myself with the officers, I no less want the perpetrator captured, even if it ends up being Mr. Hoper."

"Of course," he smiled. "They will most certainly be apprehended, and your time today has proved valuable. Now Hawkins let us converge with Gushiken, yes?"

We exited the interrogation room and left the gentleman on his own. In the overseeing room, Ms. Gushiken gave a perplexed look at how the interrogation went.

"What exactly was the point of your questions?" she asked in puzzled fashion. "From the look of it, it looks like you were just beating around the bush."

"I concur with Ms. Gushiken. I fail to see the purpose of the information you gathered there, Mr. Allegro."

"I wanted to judge his character. As you two seemed to be aware, he does not seem like a person who lets his emotions get the better of him. Instead, he prefers to stay with a poker face, so that we may not know what his thoughts and intentions are. Paying attention to his words is the best you can do with these types of people. I'm sure you can agree on that point with me, Gushiken."

"You're right, but I just can't see him being related to the killing. As of right now, there's nothing that links to him, so like I said earlier, I just can't understand why he prefers to keep his mouth shut."

My companion and I gave exchanged looks knowing the reason why he has preferred to not speak up.

"Anyhow," interjected my companion, "unless you bring him a lawyer, he's not going to break anytime soon. Plus, considering the history we share now, I don't think he's expecting to speak to me in detail anytime soon."

"First the local pub and now this. Despite all this time, you still like picking fights with anyone who acts high and mighty, huh?" she shook her head in disapproval.

"What can I say? I just like being the underdog," he shrugged in a comical, self-satisfied way.

//So, he has always been like this then...//

My companion gave a glance in my directions.

"Speaking of, I noticed you seemed distracted earlier. Did something come to mind during the interview?"

"Hm? Oh, It is nothing important."

"Well, if it's not important, feel free to share it then. What is it?"

"Well," I hesitated, "while you were speaking with the gentleman, I somehow noticed something peculiar. Underneath his fingernails, there was some sort of white substance. "

My companions ogled curiously.

"Some white substance? he asked.

"Yes."

He began thinking about this odd detail.

"Could you elaborate in detail?"

"I could not make heads or tails, but it kind of looked like the remains of some kind of dry powder. I guess the best comparison would have to be like a crushed spice you would normally use for cooking."

He started to think out loud, muttering to himself as if trying to understand.

"Hawkins, are you completely sure of what you saw?"

"I confess I am not as observant as you are, but I am definitely confidant that I saw something in his fingers."

Confused, the captain looked at us at the exchange we were having.

"Hello? Remember me? Captain of the case?"

"I have to go. There is a set of pressing matters I have to confirm. It's just a hunch but, if what you say is true, Hawkins, then we might have us the evidence that would directly pull him to the crime."

"Evidence?!" I cried.

"Wait, wait, wait, are you seriously suggesting Facsimile is involved?! That's ridiculous you saw the scene of the crime. There wasn't a link to him at all!"

"More than you care to believe, my dear Gushi. There are some details I have not shared with you yet. And for that reason, I have to follow this scent. Hawkins here will illuminate you with our findings. Make sure you wait for me until I come back. I will explain everything in the evening. Good day!"

"I knew you didn't tell me everything, you jerk!"

With great haste he rushed towards the exit, disappearing as the Chief shook her fist in great anger, cursing profoundly. She quickly glared at me, knowing that I was part of his scheme.

//Oh no.//

"E-eh?!"

"You better spill the beans right now. NOW."

Chapter 12

3rd Moon

27th Phase

2018

2:01 pm

Sharing what we had learned so far, Ms. Gushiken finally understood where our investigation had landed us. Her anger overshadowed the revelation, as she was furious over being kept in the dark.

"That jerk. I can't believe he withheld information again!"

"I apologize on his behalf. He wanted to confirm things first before he shared any more information."

"Did he tell you that?"

"Um."

"Whatever, I don't care. Here I thought he was starting to become different, but I guess he hasn't changed at all."

//Why does the air feel so awkward suddenly?//

"What do you make of the papers, then?"

"As much as a pain as he is, the dirt he dug up regarding his past presents an interesting case to be made against Facsimile. But it's not something that I can definitely say to be conclusive."

"I agree. At first, I thought it could be a stretch, but the more I thought about it the more probable it sounded."

"Any theory is probable. But if you have no evidence to support your theory, it's all fantasy and what-ifs."

"I understand. But even so, it is a possibility worth investigating."

"No, it's not."

//What?//

"What makes you think we have the time to consider 'possible' ideas? That would just be wasting everyone's time, your organization's included. We don't have time for that."

//But you are an officer! Is it not your job to get through the facts and examine every angle of the case?//

Inclined against the wall, the captain let out a resounding sigh.

"Besides, it's not like we can convince anyone with just theories. Try telling that to the judge. You'll get nowhere if you can't prove he was there, let alone did the kill. It would do you well to just ignore his incoherent rambling and just keep doing yourself-"

"So, you would rather give up and not fight? You would prefer to leave an innocent imprisoned for life than investigate every possibility? All for the sake of saving time?!" I cried in anger.

"It's not like I don't want to consider everything! I want to get this right too, dammit!"

Frustrated, she hits the wall with brute force, her fist visibly shaking.

"Then trust in us. Trust in Mr. Allegro. I know he will come through in the end. Just give him some time, please."

With my conviction, she quietly retracts her rough demeanor and softens up completely.

"I just hope you're right. Because if he doesn't, our suspect is going to be taken to court tomorrow. And by then, everything will be out of my hand."

With nothing else to do I followed Ms. Gushiken towards the rest area. With a cola in my hand, all we could do was wait, and what seemed minutes turned into hours. Boredom was beginning to take possession of me, and Ms. Gushiken was growing impatient at no new development. It was then that suddenly the familiar officers came running towards us with great urgency.

"Boss! Boss!" exclaimed the pair.

"What's the matter? Hm? Why do you guys look like you've seen a ghost-"

"The witness Allegro brought yesterday! He's gone!"

"Gone?!" we exclaimed.

"You better not be pulling my leg, or both your jobs are on the line. What do you mean, gone?"

"He's not on the chair! The room is completely empty!"

"That's absurd. His leg was handcuffed to the chair. How the hell did he get away?"

"We don't know!" they answered, taking turns in explaining. "We were doing our hourly patrol across the halls when suddenly the lad in the security room came running in a scatterbrained manner. He told us that Facsimile was not in the interrogation room and upon inspection he was right! We tried to rewind the film that had been uploaded to the cloud, but it was cut abruptly!"

"What?!"

Kicking her chair away, she ran towards the security room. Knowing what was going to happen, we decided to follow her, for the less we needed was a very angry woman berating an employee doing his job.

"You, nerd, explain, now!"

The employee gave a thorough explanation of what had happened. He observed that the camera had gone out, but he thought initially that it must have frozen its transmission. Five minutes pass and still nothing. Worried, he got up and made his way towards the interrogation room, looking through the one-sided glass window that outsiders can see through. Noticing how the detained had escaped -and the camera altogether ripped from the wall- he grew to a frenzied state and immediately ran towards the nearby officers. Stressed, he bowed and apologized for the blunder. We all three felt bad, for it was out of his control, but thanks to the scolding the captain had done to him, he felt like he had done something wrong.

"Damn it all! We got 10 officers in this detention center, and nobody saw anything!"

I knew that Ms. Gushiken struck me as a very short-tempered woman who had no room for mistakes from anyone, but she was positively ire, more so than what I had hoped to see from her. She stormed out of the hall, possibly making a call to let all officers know of his possible escape.

Knowing that calming her down would not do prove fruitful, I decided to leave her be. Directing myself to the two officers, I asked if I could investigate the room.

"I don't think there seems to be a problem, right Charles?"

"I don't think so, no. Considering you guys of the Agency have given us a helping hand so far, I don't see why not. Normally, we run this by the captain. But, as you can see well, it might not be best to ask. My mate and I must go follow her and start the search with her. If you need anything else, just talk to one of our buddies from the detention center. Other than that, cheers and good luck, Miss!"

With that, I decided to go to the last space Mr. Facsimile was occupying. Upon opening the door, I was met with an empty, silent room. I grew to ponder before anything.

//As expected, he is nowhere to be seen. I did not see him fleeing early when we were outside with Mr. Allegro, nor did Gushiken and I saw any suspicious person exit through the front door. But he could not have just disappeared. No conjurer of this day of age could prove such a feat. No, I think this must have been someone from the outside that disguised themselves as an officer. It could possibly be our fourth guest that was on the night of the killing. Calm down Hawkins, calm down. There is always an answer for everything. I just have to have a look around and apply the principles Mr. Allegro always applies.//

I decided to take a look around but came across nothing noteworthy. No visible shoe prints were left, and nothing that could serve as a clue. The camera used to be located on the southeastern wall, giving a clear view of the entire room. But alas, there was nothing, nothing but the cords that it had been pulled off from. Thinking of the alternatives, my telephone began ringing. I was being called by Ms. Okeanos.

"Hey there, Jenny!" she greeted with delight.

"Okeanos?"

"I tried calling you but you didn't answer, so I asked Raoul where you were. I just finished hooking up your Guardian to the watch, and lo-and-behold! Ta-da!"

It was a circular smartwatch that displayed the Guardian on the screen.

"I have been properly installed, Ms. Hawkins. I believe I look like humans say chic, no?" he stated with a proud expression.

"Haah, you look dashing," I replied with pain.

"It seems she is not pleased Ms. Okeanos. I thought you said this would prove to be entertaining for both of us."

"You're right. Normally she would cringe at my remarks, but she looks stressed more than anything. Is something wrong?"

"Oh, it is that dreaded Mr. Facsimile. He has escaped! We have no idea and no clue how, but the room is completely empty. With no clue, how are we supposed to know where he left off to?"

"Is that so? What about Luci?"

"He is not here. He is doing an errand related to evidence."

"I see. Well, I just finished with this baby, and I have nothing to work on. And seeing I have to give you your Guardian, I don't see why not. I shouldn't help you out."

"I appreciate the assistance, but I lack understanding how you could help me in this conundrum with nothing to work on."

"Are you serious?" shocked at the answer.

"What?"

"Did you actually forget you have a Guardian now? Just give us a minute, and we'll be there. Buh bye!"

Without letting me say a word, she hanged up.

It was not long when she arrived. She rapidly scurried along the halls until our gaze met. Noticing my glance, she hurriedly came and gave me the Guardian.

"He's all set! Here you go!"

I retrieved the Guardian accessory and, upon establishing it on my wrist, the accessory made immediate contact, rapidly making its impression on my body. I felt a sudden sting at my arm, but it was nothing too harsh. Establishing itself comfortably, the AI came out of the watch display.

"Hello. I am finally here; I hope I can be as much service as I can, Miss Hawkins."

"I appreciate it, John. But I confess that I am not sure what you will be able to do in a room without anything to go by, John."

"Well, there are a lot of things the little guy can do, but I'll throw a bone and help. John, scan the room and see if you can find anything."

"Of course, commencing a scan."

Like a hound following the command of its trainer, the AI began examining the room with a broad red light in a circular motion.

"Scanning done! it exclaimed, processing results."

"It would seem that someone else had entered the room, assisting the witness escape."

"I had an inkling of that, but how can you tell? I hardly see anything," I asked.

"The doorknob. I have scanned an unusual set of silhouettes left on them. Their figure resembles what would be fingers. And while there are no actual shoe prints inside the room, it could be that our person was wearing a pair of shoe print-less shoes."

"Shoe print-less shoes?" I asked, puzzled.

"Oh yeah! I remember hearing that some time ago. This is just a rumor, but apparently some criminals have been making some underground shoes that don't leave prints on the ground. Supposedly, it was meant to be some eco warriors meant to reduce environmental damage thanks to the CO2 and polymer attributes. Of course, the feature was a side effect from the product itself, but that didn't stop from bad guys using them to commit crimes and get away with it."

"I see. So, our perpetrators must have brought these shoes to make their escape undetected. Good thing they were careless enough to leave those markings, though. John, is it possible for you to search for who the fingerprints belong to?"

"Certainly. Scanning. Done. Researching on the cloud. Done. Error search failed. No such person exists."

"Well, that's weird."

"Maybe John is still updating?"

"No, no, I made sure his operating system was all up to date with the latest version."

"Then there is foul play."

"That, or perhaps someone else, deleted the information from the network. Whichever the case, for someone claiming to be innocent, someone sure does know very interesting people."

We were feeling uncomfortable. How someone had entered the room without nobody noticing, how they left little to no trace and how our second person had no identity to speak of, meant that they were no ordinary person. It could be that someone or some organization had aided his escape.

"Whatever the case," I broke silence, "We can at least conclude that they must have gotten a sort of disguise as well as some tools to remain undetected."

"Why do you think that?"

"Well, how else could they have gotten inside? For example, if someone were to infiltrate the Agency, surely no one would blink an eye. Putting certain key figures aside like Mr. or even Ms. Gushiken, no one would notice unless they did a check."

"You do have a point. And that would make sense when you consider no red flags were reported."

"Agreed."

"So, what do we do?"

Pondering, I began to think of alternatives in tracking down our rescuer and suspicion.

//This is tough. With no shoe prints to go by, we cannot exactly locate them. There may not be any shoe prints in the building, but what if there was a way to track them? What if..."

"Hm, John, is it possible to trace where they went based on the silhouette left by mud, for example?"

"That is doable. So long as I have a silhouette to go by, the rest is easily tracked."

"Ah, I get it!" exclaimed my friend.

"Even if we cannot find any shoe prints, we can still find traces of dirt on the ground left by them."

"You're a genius! Then what are we waiting for? Let's go outside!"

Following my suggestion, we made our way towards the entrance, and we were left with the same murky floor from when we arrived.

"Perfect, and they are still relatively fresh, which makes it easier to read. John, if you cou-"

"Wait! How about I do it this time? Charlie, do your thing!"

"Certainly! Commencing scan Connecting to global satellite to measure distance Processing Done! I have detected two traces starting from here. They go for fifteen miles. Their stride was quick, so they must have been walking quickly."

"Aw, nice job little guy, I'm so proud of you!"

"Yay!!"

"Hehe, send those coordinates to my friend here, okay?"

"Done! Sending..."

"Receiving..." uttered my small contraption. "Received. A path has been made."

With the routealready set, we boarded Mr. Raoul's vehicle and instructed him the directions.In no less than ten minutes, we arrived and were met with an old, abandoned-house. The windows were shot down. ivies were enveloping the rusticarchitecture with moss growing from the roof as the droplets of water fell ontothe overgrown grass. The main gate was decrepit. What remained of what seemedto be statues were left in a state of eternal broken. The statue wasundecipherable and undesirable. The gate was boarded up with ironed out woodplanks that have gotten soft thanks to the humid weather this country is wontto be. Finally, the sign that belonged to the original residents of this househas been scratched, making it not visible to understand. Indeed, it was aclassic description of an old abode damaged by the power of time.

Chapter 13

3rd Moon

27th Phase

2018

2:55 pm

"Well, this sure looks homey," said sarcastically my blue friend.

"By the look of it, it seems this place has been left abandoned."

"Sure, looks like it. So, this is the place, then?"

"From the look of it, yes. The track stops on the curbside, so my guess is that they must be inside somewhere."

"That makes sense. Shouldn't we wait for Luci to join us, though? We're going to be dealing with some bad people, so it wouldn't hurt to wait for backup."

"No," I adamantly answered. "if we wait any longer, there is a chance that Mr. Facsimile and his cohorts escape before we can detain them. It would be prudent to avoid anymore damaged caused by the party. Besides, Mr. Allegro is right now finding the last pieces of evidence. If we can find him before he comes back, it will only make everything go smoothly for everyone involved in this case. So long as Mr. Allegro finds the clue needed to connect him, then it is checkmate for him."

My companion sighed.

"Guess I can't stop you when your mind is made up then, huh? I just hope we don't get into trouble by going on our own though. Raoul, make sure you have the car ready in case we have to make a run for it."

"Of course. I will be waiting here in case you need me. I pray for both your safety. Good luck."

We approached the entrance gate in a cautious manner. Upon inspection, it became evident that the lock had been tampered with, confirming that both the escapee and rescuer had gotten inside with great haste. If we were to enter, then this would be a point of no return. Not because we were breaking and entering. But because we were going to be experiencing a dangerous encounter with two cunning criminals, that clearly will do anything to escape the law. But my conviction was stronger than my fears, and so I pressed onward. Five steps ahead, however, I realized that my friend was still at the entrance, looking deadpan at me.

"Er, Okeanos? Are you alright?" I asked.

"No, nothing, just here admiring the scenery of this abandoned, decrepit house where there's a chance that the criminals might be lurking in the shadows, ready to kill! Jenny, did you think of going inside without anything to protect yourself!?"

"What do you mean? I am aware that my Guardian possesses the weapon feature. I should be fine in due time."

"In due time? Oh my, well, do you know how to activate it?"

"Voice command?"

My friend groaned as she buried her face between her hands.

"And here I thought you were going to be the cautious one, but you're just as reckless as Luci!" she cried.

"Alright, listen up! For you to use your weapon, you need to establish contact it. Simply touching your accessory is fine. After that, you have to concentrate and visualize the weapon you'll be using. For first timers, the first weapon that comes into mind will be yours when you're ready to summon it. After that, you're stuck with that, so even if you try to picture in your mind a different type of weapon it won't spawn because your Guardian can only retain one. Having a weapon as is puts maximum strain on the body, so imagine having different kinds. You'll just explode, kablooey!"

"Kablooey. I understand what you said, but you sure have a way of explaining things. Well, here goes nothing."

Closing my eyes, I concentrated on manifesting my chosen weapon. After a few seconds, I saw it: a lone semi-automatic revolver in the middle of the room. It bears a striking modern design that had hints of customized parts that seem reminiscence of things you would witness on TV space operas. It was an interesting design to say the least, however, and after some delay, I picked it up with my right hand. Suddenly I returned to where I stood, and a few flashing lights emanated from the watch that Okeanos had built for me, transforming into the same revolver that I had created in my mind.

"What the? "How in the devil?!" I exclaim in astonishment.

"Wow! With decal and everything is nice! Normally, I would spare some of your time on explaining the science behind it, but right now we don't have time. Do you have your weapon cocked and set to non-Lethal? There should be a switch somewhere. Try checking on the grip on the side."

After some delay, I found the switch she had described. With a twist on the switch, the gun buzzed and changed forms.

"Good, everything is set. This will be your first time, so try to wing it until you get training regarding using your guardian weapon."

"Wing it?"

"You know. Improvise."

"Improvise? At a time like this?"

"Hey, it's not my fault you decided to go gung-ho without considering you would be chasing criminals unarmed, hello?" she declared with contempt in her voice.

//I hate it when she is right.//

"Touché. Then what about yours, Okeanos? Where is your weapon?"

Without a second to spare, her necklace started to glow, and out of it, came what looked to be a type of staff, roughly a bit smaller than her size."

"I don't have that much stamina compared to the trained investigators, but I can still give some backup. My guardian weapon is equipped with some advanced elemental particles, such as hydrogen, oxygen, nitrogen, and carbon. With it, I can create some awesome weather effects to help out."

"Fascinating! So, like a wizard of sorts?

"If you mean a wiz on science, then hell yeah," she responded with a confident smile.

"Sure, heh. Well, here goes nothing."

"Right behind you!"

Equipped with our weapons, we made our way towards the lone courtyard. A washed-up garden was in the middle, collecting dust and moss on the marble statue, as the water was contaminated profusely. Even though my friend was wary of our eerie surroundings, I was left excited exploring this abandoned building. The gloomy atmosphere, the thrill of the hunt and the weapon at hand proved to be enough to make my eyes shine in enjoyment. It felt invigorating to experience this, making me think of Father and all the adventures he would tell me after bed.

We entered the main building and were met with some abandoned photographs around the lobby entrance. Scattered on the ground, the broken photographs were possibly left by the original owner of the house. Trying to avoid making unnecessary sound, we traversed through the lobby and before us came some scattered debris, with a set of stairs to the side of it. A few steps missing, and a few steps broken. Carefully ascending them, we made some notes on where to place our steps, dancing so that we may not suffer a fall. Finally, I carefully extended my hand, so that Okeanos had no problems climbing with ease. Once we had completed the exercise, we continued our trail. A creeped and decayed corridor was left unattended, connecting us to the main hall with only a few walks away.

Proceeding inside a faint voice that could be heard from where we were. From the distance, it became clear that it was coming from the end of this stretched corridor. It was the voice of a man, undoubtedly the voice of Mr. Facsimile. Hunched down, staying close to the nearby walls, we tried to make our presence as unknown as possible. Okeanos caught the wind as well and positioned herself next to me, against the wall. Retracting something from her pocket, she picked up an earpiece she had with herself and, -with a push on the button- an antenna had come out from it. Commanding her Guardian, she directed its attention towards the noise. Cautiously, we slowly got closer until Ms. Okeanos took a hold of me and signaled that we were fine with the distance. Then, picking up the sound from the antenna, she shared with me another earphone she had linked her Guardian with me, so that I was not to miss any of the dialogue that was taking place.

"I must thank you, friend," said the criminal in a delighted tone.

"I was not expecting for this to go as smoothly as it went. Pinning the crime on that fool was cunning on my part, and with no evidence to connect me to it, I dare say this was a perfect crime."

He laughed, enjoying the moment at the outcome.

"I appreciate your assistance, though, really. I know how he has a no innocent involved policy, but really, who here is innocent? The blood he carried was a sin in itself. And Hoper proved to be a fool when he crossed me, blindly following his master's bidding. He had it coming. I must say, however, that you really have not lost a second of training. How you managed to dodge the officers and tamper without traces at the scene of the crime is impressive. I remembered you used to be a cold-blooded killer, but it would seem you have grown significantly in all areas of the field. In due part, thanks to him, I am sure. This calls for a drink then."

With that, he retrieved a small flask he had hidden from his back pocket and poured some alcohol on two glasses he had placed on the table beside him.

"To a successful business, cheers."

"That's him right, Jenny? The guy you were chasing yesterday?"

"Yes, it is him. It looks like he is with his rescuer. They seem to be hiding in the shadows, however, for I cannot catch a glimpse of them."

"You're right. I can't see who they're talking to."

"Do you believe we should grow closer to get a better look?"

"We could. But any closer we get to them will make us become more visible, making it possible for us to be spotted."

//Confound it all.//

"Nothing like a good old glass of Mouvedre. Hm? What, you don't drink? Come drink up. What reason would I have to poison you? What poison I had made was dealt to Primo."

The woman stepped out of the shadow and picked up her drink. Her face became visible as some of the light penetrating the skylight slightly illuminated her. Her figure was average and lean, and her crimson-colored eyes were the only feature of her that even in darkness could be seen as clear as day. She was covered with a face mask that hid her face, covered in a silky, battered hood. She was dressed urban like, with an overbearing jacket and skinny jeans. Her hair was tied in a traditional tosonian fashion, her bangs only escaping from her beautiful ebony hair, as her mystery only grew more.

"Good right? Only with you I would be sharing the finest wine in the country. After all, with what history we share, it is the least I could do."

"You did tell him about this operation, right?" she spoke in a low tone.

"Don't worry about the small details. Besides, we'd be doing him a favor, considering Primo was also a scum of society."

"You better. Or else you're gonna get it."

"Heh, threats mean nothing to me. It would seem that you still haven't changed your dog like mentality," said Mr. Facsimile in a dry ridiculing tone.

"And it would seem you still haven't earned enough IQ points ever since you left us."

"Tch. Still running your mouth, aren't you? Well, no matter, once I escape, I'll have nothing to do with any of you and this God forsaken country."

Finishing his glass, he places it on a nearby wooden crate.

"Tch, let's get a move on. Better to move now than later."

"Of course. Before we leave, however..."

She gazed towards Facsimile as he made his way towards a bundle of gas cans that was safely tucked in in the corner of the room.

"What are you plotting now?"

"'Vengeance is a dish best served cold'. Heh, a very intriguing saying, don't think? It states that with time, one can easily execute their most malevolent plans, for success favors the cautious ones. As their victim has lowered their guard and has reached a perfected state of execution, I believe that when planned, anything can be done. And after all these years, working for that dastard has finally paid off."

With a match in his hand, he strikes it against his cuff. A burning light manifested itself as the dancing flame stole Facsimile's attention.

"Death is rewarding, but not satisfying. Like a bandage, it only covers the wound. So, if a bandage does not do the job, then simply add salt. I am the salt, and like a wound, the sins of the Primos will be purged. Having plagued hundreds of victims throughout the last century, everyone was bound to their chains. And after experiencing this firsthand, I then knew this was my calling. Nothing like a fitting way to repay that accursed 100-Year-Old Debt."

With a flick, he threw the match on where the gas stood and cast a fire.

"This guy's insane! He's planning to burn this frigging place down!" whispered my companion.

"To what end? What does he get from burning such a place down?

The assassin stood quietly, staring down at her companion.

"Let us be off. The deed is done, and I don't plan for us to get burned. This abandoned place will be nothing more but a burnt memory, along with the rest of the Cugini name."

Everything felt like something out of play. The falling debris, the growing ember, and the villains escaping as they had finished their objective, satisfied with the outcome. My teeth clenched in excitement, knowing full that it was now or ever. Driven by my impulses, I uttered some words that resonated through the walls of the room.

"Not If I have anything to say about that! Hold it!"

"Jenny, what are you doing?!"

Gripping my weapon tightly, I came out of the shadows, aiming high towards our culprit.

Chapter 14

3rd Moon
27th Phase
2018
4:00 pm

Astonished by our arrival, his face contorted itself. The fake smile was now gone. Anger was the only thing that crossed his face, knowing full well that his escape was in jeopardy.

"And, like a mosquito, they keep coming back. How the devil did you know we were here?"

"That is unimportant. Slowly raise your hand and do not even think about moving, both of you."

Her eyes affixed towards me, she glared in my direction. As her penetrating crimson eyes stared into my soul, I grew anxious, for I did not know what I was to expect from the person Mr. Allegro had alluded to.

"No one needs to get hurt. So please, no sudden movements."

At my words, she cocked her head with contempt in her eyes, questioning the words I had commanded. Glimpsing at Okeanos, she finally understood the situation of the room.

"Ah, I see. You had help from your friend there to track us down. No doubt the Collective Detective Agency sent their pawns after us."

How she had deduced all that was beyond me. Clearly, we were dealing with someone more than just a simple killer. I was growing relatively nervous, for I did not expect for these unprecedented developments to take place. However, a look at my friend was all I needed to steel my nerves. Her grip towards her weapon, her curled brows and her hunch posture exemplified a display of determination. Her expression was not shattered, and she was even more focused on stopping these criminals than ever before.

"Well," chuckled my friend, "at least our reputation is growing. I was starting to grow worried for a second there."

"Don't flatter yourself. No normal person would have access to the Guardian system. Besides us, you people are the only ones who have access to it."

//Besides us?//

"Really now? Now that's interesting!" remarked my companion." Well, how about we have a little chat over it, then? We could compare data, share research notes-"

Her katana soon appeared out of thin air, directing her blade towards our directions.

"I don't have time for jokes. Either walk away or die."

"Yeah, no, thanks. I'd rather take my chances and bring both of you behind bars. Last warning, drop your weapon now."

Mr. Facsimile, aware of his chances, directs his remark towards his accomplice.

"It would seem that running is out of the question. Would you mind showing them what you're worth?"

She gave a very deadpan look towards him.

"I don't need you to tell me what to do. Besides, it's not like you can't fight."

"I would if I still had my weapon. Besides, I'm a chemist, not a fighter."

"Tch. Even for that, you're still useless. Whatever, just don't get in my way."

With her warning, Mr. Facsimile could not help but smile gleefully. Taking note that it was going to get perilous, he went to the sides, to not to not get in the middle of the action.

"I gave you a warning, and you didn't take it. Don't blame me for what happens next, pawns."

With her threat, we readied our ourselves and prepared ourselves for the confrontation."

"Well, guess negotiations out of the window. Guess we're going to have to buckle down, right Jenny? Jenny?"

// I am shaking in my boots right now! At first this seemed like the right choice but now at the moment of truth I am not so sure! I do not even know what I'm supposed to do! I can't leave these killers go, but I also do not want to die here! what kind of person would that make me?//

As these thoughts of self-doubt began weighing on me, the recollection of the past became to appear on mind:

"Daddy, you're late!"

"Sorry sunflower, daddy just had work and had to go to the doctor."

"Mommy!"

"What is it, Jennifer? Oh, hi there dear, why, good heavens, what happened to you?!"

Daddy is hurt! He said he had to go to the doctor!"

"I am sure he is exaggerating dear, you know how he is wont to. Why, goodness John, what happened?!"

"I'm sorry. I know I promised I wasn't going to do anything reckless, but some of the officers and I were chasing someone. We caught him, but I regrettably caught a bullet in the chest in the process."

"Oh dear. Well, did they take it out at least?"

"Unfortunately, no. They said they'd notify me when to pass by to do the operation."

"The mediocrity in today's doctors. If I had the chance, I could have possibly taken it out perfectly!" she said annoyed.

"Waaah!!!"

"H-hey, your dad isn't going anywhere! It's just a scratch, see?"

"Waaah!!!"

"John!"

"W-what?!"

"Honestly. You know well you should not be showing those bruises to her."

"Is that so?"

"Sometimes I am amazed how much of a dunce you can be."

"And sometimes I'm amazed at how the years haven't stopped you from being mean."

" I do not w-want d-daddy to die!"

"Oof! If you keep hitting me like that, daddy might die!"

"John!"

"I'm joking! I'm joking! Now, now Jennifer, I am not going to die anytime soon. This smarts a bit, but it had to happen for the greater good."

"Greater good?"

"Mhm. If your old man didn't intervene there, some people would have died. I did come off injured, but I'm still here, am I not?"

"But I don't care about those people. I only care about you!"

He gave a soft smile and petted my small, soft head.

"And I'm sorry for making you worry. But sometimes we have to do dangerous things if we want to protect the things we love. If I had not stopped those criminals, then they would have continued their reign of terror, and keep doing wicked things to the people. They might have done bad things to your mother and you. You know, I sometimes get scared when I do dangerous things."

"You do? But you are so brave!"

"Heh, well, I can be brave sometimes. But I can also get scared too. I am not perfect, but you do know what helps me?"

"What?"

"I think of you, my little sunflower. You give me the reason to keep doing what I do. So, I want you to do the same whenever you feel scared as well. Always think of the things you wish to protect."

Returning to the present, my resolve grew from within.

//That is right, I came here looking for these criminals in order to protect the people and stop the killings. This is not the time to start overthinking my decisions nor feeding my fears! I became an investigator not to only to follow the footsteps of Father but also help people in need! If I let them go, then it would have been for nothing! No, I refuse!//

With my newfound determination, I aim down on sight towards the assassin and take a shot at her. Seeing the incoming fire, she moves her face to the side, dodging comfortably without any hesitation.

"Jenny..." she mumbled in shock.

In silence, I glare intently at our opponent, not paying mind to the words of my friend.

"I gave you a way out and you rejected. Your stupidity will be your downfall now. Die."

Without a notice, she lunged herself, commencing her attack without warning. I had grown unaware of her speed until I realized by a second how close she had gotten to my face.

"Don't just stand there, get out of the way!' cried my companion.

Recalling my senses, I grew to see the attack, barely dodging all in one piece. Like the wind, the upward slash she had done left only a small cut below the eye. It was then that what she said was true, and I realized that her intent was to kill with all her might.

I fell and rolled towards Ms. Okeanos, shameful of my pitiful display.

"My apologies. I thought I had for sure gotten the hit."

"Don't worry about it. Just get up and stay sharp. Considering she almost left you blind there, she's aiming to end it here quick."

"Should we take a more aggressive approach?"

"I think so. We're not dealing with a normal thug now, anyway. Set your Guardian to Lethal and make sure you count your shots."

"Right!"

With a twist on the dial, my gun had transformed. Although it was a slight modification, the contents of the weapon had changed appearance, the chamber now filled with what seemed to be bullets filled with electrical shots.

"Finally showing your fangs then? Good. Make it interesting at least.."

Once again, she lunged herself unto us, preparing to make her strike. Anticipating her attack, I dodged her onslaught completely and fired four consecutive shots in her directions. It was met with failure, for she had swiftly dodged all the traces I had launched, barely scratching her attire. With a hop, she drew her blade until she realized a lightning strike had come to be between us. With a backflip, she withdrew, avoiding the impending attack.

"Ah shoot, almost!" she cried.

" Four shots and she still dodged them all. Curses! There's no end to her speed!"

"Then we just keep attacking then!"

With a flick of her staff, small particles began to group up, and out of it came a cloud, rumbling in its thunderous roar. Several lightning strikes occurred in the room, all directed towards our opponent. She had grown used to the strikes, predicting each of them individually. Clearly, her senses were superior in every way imaginable, making it look like a child could do it.

I fired my two remaining shots but failed to land on my target. With a flick of the wrist, I quickly reloaded my virtual chamber with six additional ammunitions. Still, with even all that we were firing away, we were left still at a standstill. With my friend growing visibly exhausted and myself feeling the effects of my weapon, I knew that this was becoming a losing fight.

//Curses, if we keep this up, we might not make it to see it alive. Are we doomed to fail here? Is there not a way to turn this around? Think, Hawkins think!//

As I look around, I noticed Okeanos barely holding back the assassin's attack, staff in both hands, holding her with her back against the wall.

"Ngh. I'm getting fried."

"Disappointing. I thought that it would prove to be interesting the kind of people the Agency has now been adopting."

Kicking Okeanos's staff away, she proceeded to hit her with a solid kick to her cheek towards the side, leaving her exhausted and beaten, covered with blood. Finding the strength to get up, she falls pitifully, for she was too tired in due part to her low stamina.

"Master! Please, you have to get up!" exclaimed her Guardian.

"I'm sorry Charlie. I think I'm down for the count. Jenny..."

"Okeanos!"

"In the end, I couldn't be much help. I'm sorry for letting you down..."

As she mustered her last words, she fell to the floor and passed out, unconscious of everything.

"Looks like this was too much for her. Don't worry, I'll make sure to end it quick."

She firmly raises her blade to the sky, preparing her final blow to strike her down.

//No! Okeanos!//

Urgency was all that I felt. I had forgotten all my senses and was unaware of my surroundings. All I could see was my poor friend resigning to her fate at the hands of the woman who had been a thorn for us.

//I cannot leave her there. No, I will not! What kind of private investigator would I be if I could not even save one life? No, I refuse!//

I felt a glimmer in my eye and inside my body blazed a burning flame, with the will to see through these impending walls. With no time to think, I centered my gaze one more time towards my target. Accounting everything to save my friend, I pulled the trigger and fired. As soon as she was in the middle of her swing, the shot penetrated her hand, leaving her immobilized from the attack. Slowly, looking towards her hands, droplets of blood fell from her palm.

"I haven't bled in years. And yet this stray managed to do so."

She glared in my directions.

"You have piqued my curiosity. I would have love to see what more you would be capable if put into a corner. However, I grow bored at this and I want to this to be over. So,"

Her eyes glowing, she gets on a stance ready to launch herself.

"I'll make this as quick as possible for both of you. Die."

As she ran with upmost haste, floating with great speed, I panicked. Reloading my weapon, I fired everything I could muster, but I was met with failure, cutting every bullet I had thrown. My stamina faltering, I fell to my knee, not having the energy to continue the fight. She slowly approached me, looked down with some contempt in her eyes.

"Stop playing with your food and finish her already!" Facsimile interjected. "May I remind you that we are in a burning building?!"

With indifference on her face, she scoffed and raised her blade towards the heavens.

"Goodnight."

Knowing that I had lost, and that there was no other help to come to us thanks to my brash decision-making, I had resigned my fate to her. with nothing else, I closed my eyes, hoping that it was quick and not painful.

//I guess... I guess this is as far as my journey goes. Mother, Father, forgive me...//

Just as she had tried to do earlier, she swung her sword downwards. Expecting my life to end here, however, a sudden sharp metallic sound filled the room. Not understanding why I had not met my fate yet, I hesitantly slowly opened my eyes, realizing that my partner, Lucio Allegro, was holding her blade back with all his might. To my shock, she grew to be surprised at the outcome of who her new opponent was.

"What?!"

Chapter 15

3rd Moon

27th Phase

2018

4:51 pm

With everything solved, we decided to stop by the Detention Center to inform everything that had transpired to Mr. Hoper and Ms. Gushiken.

Anxiously waiting for the development in his cell, Mr. Allegro assured him that everything had been taken care of and that he was to be a free man soon enough.

"Good heavens, thank you!" he clamored. "I still can't believe he did the deed, but I'm just grateful that you got that dreadful scoundrel. To think he hired an assassin, only for him to do the deed. What convoluted madness!"

I happily nodded.

"Agreed. I am not sure I can keep up with everything happening so quick. But still, It sure is good that everything worked out. Mystery solved!"

"Not everything," said my astute companion.

"Huh?"

"The deal you and the victim spoke of. It was his inheritance, wasn't it?"

Deadpanned and quiet, he let out a piteous smile.

"I take it Facsimile told you."

"No, I found out about it on my own."

"Inheritance sir?" I asked.

"After I went to the coroner's, I decided to give a quick call to McKenzie and ask some small questions regarding the Primo family. I asked if he had next of kin who would inherit his gains and residency, as the police could not find any will to speak of. He told me that he had once a wife but that she had passed away to a disease from the heart at an early age. Besides his attendants, he spent his life in solitude, for he didn't have friends or family to begin with. He was the last bastion of the Primo family. So, what does he decide to do? He gives it to Hoper. Why? Because he caught wind regarding Facsimile's plot."

"He did? How?"

"Primo was a man who could read people's intention. And while I'm not sure when he found out about it, it was obvious that the man had seen past his deceitful smile, plotting something to kill him. At his current age and condition, he knew that there was no way to stop him from dying. His health, Facsimile, he did not care. He knew that death was near. Which is why he took immediate action: He entrusted his fortune, residency and last name to his beloved right-hand man, Mr. Jeffrey Hoper. In disbelief at the ludicrous request, you got furious and got in a discussion with him, sensing that he was soon to perish and that he had given up the will to continue fighting. Everyone became aware of the issue, but they could understand what the issue was, thanks in due part to the soundproof walls. I have mostly deduced everything, but you're welcomed to correct me if I got something wrong."

Mr. Hoper, glancing at us shares a pained smile.

"You people really are nothing short of amazing. It is as you said, it was about his inheritance."

"You knew about his incoming death, didn't you?"

Defeated, recollecting his last moments with the victim, he clasps his knees in frustration.

"His expression, his physical appearance, it was all too noticeable. Some of my coworkers noticed as well and relayed what they had observed towards, thinking that he was to meet an unfortunate end by some old enemy of his past. As his confidant, I grew worried, for he was mostly a jovial man throughout the establishment. I tried to confront him after he was done with Facsimile. Seeing if I could help him, I offered my services in any way possible. But he just waved me off and told me that it was useless for me to do anything and that a young man such as I should not be involved in his affairs. He was never one to dissuade my assistance. On the contrary, he always welcomed any help his employees offered wholeheartedly. But the man I once knew was gone, and all I saw was a shell marching into his final breath. I insisted on my services once again, but he refused with anger. So, I in frustration, I raised my voice and the rest you already know. I knocked a few things, but what else was I supposed to do? My friend was going to die, and I was powerless. I'm sure you would grow furious if a friend of yourself was going to die at your eyes, and you could do nothing."

Mr. Allegro softened his display.

"But," I interjected, "you did do something. You helped us capture the criminal and avenge your fallen friend. And not only that, but thanks to your testimony, you helped protect the lives of all the people that Mr. Facsimile had blackmailed. You have a good heart, Mr. Hoper, and I am sure that is the reason he wanted to spare you from this family affair or any additional pain than what you already have."

I caught a glimpse of Mr. Allegro looking at my directions, his once despondent look melting away, a soft smile now crossing his face.

"Hawkins is right, Hoper. You have done your part, and I'm happy to see that the dastard has been caught red-handed away from causing further harm."

"You two..."

"Ah, right? How could I forget?"

Searching his outer pockets, he retracted a written piece of paper.

"I think this is yours."

Given to him, he only lasted one second until he realized who had written the address.

"T-this! This is his will! How on earth did you get this?!"

"Everyone has their own secrets," he said coyly. "I can tell you, however, that this is genuine. He wrote it a few minutes before he was killed by Facsimile."

"He left a will before he died. What a mad man! Well, go on, read it!" I exclaimed joyfully.

With hesitance in his voice, he recited the content of the letter:

My dear Hoper,

I know what I am asking of you may be too much for you. And I apologize for not being able to tell you everything, for I think that would put you in jeopardy, as well with McKenzie and your coworkers. I wish to leave you everything I own at your hands. I know nobody as kind and upright as you have shown this old fool, and I once again apologize for what I might possibly put you after today. Furthermore, I simply hope this will serve as a form of atonement. What I would do to be another day with everyone. You all have become my second family, and I am more than happy to know that when I am gone, I will be missed. I know now that I have been blessed, and that despite my rotten family blood flowing through me, I still did a bit of good for everyone. As for Facsimile, I do not blame the lad. My family has been damaging people's lives for more than a hundred years. I do not blame him for wanting to take my life, it is the least I could do for him. So please, do not hold any ill will towards Facsimile. Do it for me, my friend. I can only blame the cursed 100-Year-Old Debt they putted in his family. I have no regrets and have no problem with the path I had chosen. Hoper, my son, my friend, please treat everyone with the same kindness you showed me and everyone in the house. And let this new legacy live through generations to come with the hope of your capable hand. I hear some footsteps approaching.

It is probably Facsimile here, more than ready to off me. I wish you good luck and desire for you to have everlasting happiness, more than this old fool has ever had.

Sincerely yours,

Victor Primo

At the content of this letter, I could not help but grow watery at this very heartwarming exchange of words. Mr. Hoper, filled with catharsis, starts crying, droplets falling from his eyes as he read the words of his late friend.

"That selfish old fool," he whispered. "Even in death, he still decided everything on his own."

After those words, I extended him a napkin, where he happily cleaned his tears.

"Thank you, from the bottom of my heart. You two have shown to be exceptionally genius, and you have done so much for me. I still have a lot to do before I ever get close to my friend's stature. But I know that so long as I stay true to myself, it will all work out in the end."

At those words, I could not help but shed a tear, moved by what he felt. Mr. Allegro turned around trying to put up a strong front, but it came evident he was happy as well at the sudden turn of events.

"The process will take a few days, but I'm sure you'll be a free man soon enough. If you ever need any of our assistance, again feel free to give the Agency a call. Be sure to say Allegro sent you."

"Of course! Oh, and if you ever need something or need a representative in court, let me know! I'll do my best to help you two or the Agency!"

"I will keep it in mind," said Mr. Allegro in a satisfied tone. "Come along now, Hawkins, we have to reconvene with Gushi."

"Right!"

With a bow and a goodbye, we marched through the door through the main lobby where the familiar Captain, Ms. Gushiken, approached us.

"Everything is taken care of," she exposed with a sense of relief.

"Excellent. What of Facsimile?"

"We managed to arrest Facsimile. He lawyered up, so my boys will take it from here and follow up with the protocols. I have an officer inside the room until the court date, so everything should work out this time."

"Naturally."

"But still, thanks for letting me know about everything. If it wasn't for you, I think we might have screwed this one up as well."

//Ms. Gushiken...//

"Think nothing of it. We're just grateful you came through."

"Yeah, well, your friend here reminded me that it's alright to look at different angles every now and then."

"Did she now?"

"H-heh."

She gave a visible smile, knowing how, despite the differences she has with Mr. Allegro, she counts with a very reliable person to solve cases.

" I heard what happened to Okeanos. Is she going to be okay?

"We believe so," I replied.

"We are planning to take her to the doctor, but so far she just looks like she's exhausted by the action today."

"I see."

Knowing that she was going to be alright, she shares a sigh. I surmise that she had was frustrated that she was not there to help us. Noticing, my companion quickly tried to lighten her unnecessary guilt.

"Hey," he remarked. "Don't ponder over it, Gushi. Even if we had told you about the sudden development, by the time it would have been too late. So don't think about it too much."

"I guess."

Following his suggestion, she changed topics.

"We were told you guys spotted someone else besides Facsimile when you guys fought inside the building. Could you describe who they were?"

Ready to explain, my companion gave me a pat on my shoulder, as if trying to take the lead.

"No, we have no idea. It was so sudden that I couldn't get a clear picture of-"

"You're lying," she quickly uttered.

"Why would I lie?"

"Because you're hiding something. You've always been terrible at lying."

"Is that so? I thought I had gotten better through the years."

I chuckled a bit at the interaction.

"Honestly, you can be such an idiot sometimes."

"In any case, well done. Another case popped into the cabinet file; wouldn't you say?" he said with his hands stuffed in his pockets.

"Yeah. Now's the job for the D.A. to do their job. But with all the evidence we have collected and the testimonies from you lot, it shouldn't take more than two weeks. How you manage to always find these pieces of evidence is beyond me, Lucio."

"Was that a compliment? And to think you didn't like me!" he mocked with a sardonic smile.

"Hm."

//She still doesn't like you, Mr. Allegro...//

"Yeah, yeah, whatever dweeb. As for you."

She gave a fierce gaze towards me.

"Y-yes?"

"My boys told me what you did when I left. I know that you people use gadgets and whatnot to help make the process go easier, but I was surprised by that sharp thinking of yours. Sure you pursued him without backup,-which was kinda stupid if I'm honest- but you did it knowing full well that this was the only way to save Hoper."

"I-I just did what I thought was right. I apologize for not letting you know."

"Heh, yeah well, you're lucky it worked out in the end. Terrific job Hawkins."

It was unexpected to receive praise from an officer, let alone the captain. So, knowing from someone from the law gives me praise for my abrasive and logical actions made me feel happy, as if I had done something right. I grew sheepish, to which Ms. Gushiken smiled in response.

"You got a good one, Lucio. Make sure you don't screw it up. If you ever need anything, Hawkins, here's my number. I'm mostly busy during the week, so I would appreciate if you contacted me during the weekend. Anyway, have a good evening."

And with that, the captain waved her hand as she coolly walked towards her fellow officers, ready to give them further order.

"Well, I believe that we should return to the Agency, yes?" I asked.

"Yes. Considering we have to take Okeanos to the doctor, we should march onward. Plus, it would give us time to introduce you to the Director as well."

"The Director?"

"As I stated, he just got back. He should be in his office doing some work. Come, let us not waste time."

Chapter 16

3rd Moon

27th Phase

2018

5:15 pm

Upon arriving at the Agency, we were introduced to the medical doctor. A handsome gentleman in his late twenties, he was the person Mr. Allegro was alluding to, quietly cleaning his space before retiring for the day.

"Good evening, Jayr! Getting ready to clock out, I see. I trust I'm not bothering you with my timing?"

"You are. But considering you have made it a habit, I have grown used to your last-minute check-ups," he said, amused.

"But of course! I would choose no other doctor if it wasn't you, Jayr! For who would tend to my daily wounds in a delicate manner?"

Banter ensuing, I decide to bring Okeanos in, carefully carrying her to the recovery bed.

"I suppose that I could make some time. What seems to be the problem? Wait, good heavens, is that Okeanos? What on Terra happened to her?"

"It's a long story, but she got mixed in a case I was working on. She exhausted all her energy during an encounter we had, so she passed out."

The doctor eyed into my direction in a curious fashion.

"I see, poor girl. Here, let me run some diagnostics and tend to her wounds and."

Finishing his diagnostics, the doctor applies some ointments and bandages to tend to the scratches and cuts obtained from our battle. Seeing that there were no major concerns, the doctor eases up and shares what he could find.

"Her heart rate is stable, and nothing seems to be broken. There are no indications of suffering stress on the body, minus the wounds inflicted on her. Her brain is just tired, so I am guessing that with enough rest she will be good as new. I estimate that in a day or two, she will be back to normal."

"That's good to hear. Thank you Jayr."

"Thank you, doctor."

At the good news, I let out a sigh, my worries drifting away at the news. As the doctor had removed his gloves and stethoscope, he came close to my direction and inspected me with curiosity.

" You seem to be suffering from a few wounds as well. Please let me tend to your wounds."

"O-oh. Thanks. Sorry to trouble you."

"Not at all. Think nothing of it."

He was a tall man whose white coat enveloped his entire body. With a brown vest and a white dress shirt, he dressed like a modern-day gentleman, as the pocket watch gave him a sense of nobility.

"I am guessing that you must have gotten those injuries the same way as Okeanos. Well, just give me a second and you will be as good as new. I do not seem to recognize you, though. Who do I have the pleasure in talking to?" he asked with his emerald penetrating eyes.

"E-eh, you seem too close to me, sir."

"Right, my manners. Jayr, she's the recruit the Director was talking about."

"Oh?"

"Jennifer Hawkins sir. Pleasure to meet you."

"Ah! Of course, of course! It is so good to meet you! My name is Jayr Warwick, MD for the Collective Detective Agency."

"It is a pleasure to meet you, Mr. Warwick."

"Please, call me by my name. No need for formalities!" he smiled kindly. "When I was told that we were getting a new colleague, I was intrigued who we were getting. I'm surprised you were assigned to work under Lucio, though."

"And what's that supposed to mean, friend?"

"What ever you make of it, my friend. He might seem a bit rough at first, but you will learn that he is more sentimental than he lets out."

"I believe you've said enough, Jayr. I don't want her getting any wrong ideas."

"Ha-ha, if u say so."

Despite recently meeting the doctor, my impressions of him were favorable. Professional and dutiful. As expected from someone who works in the medical field.

"And you are good to go. If you ever require treatment for your injuries, you are more than welcome to come down here to get yourself checked up."

"Of course! Thank you, sir!"

"Heh. Well, I think it is high tide you did your first report with the Director. A recruit like you should speak with the man upstairs, considering he just got back from his trip."

Glancing at my unconscious friend, I stand idle, not sure what to do.

"She will be fine. My shift might be over, but we have a nurse working overnight. She will be monitored and not left alone, so you need not worry. Just focus on recuperating. Same goes to you Lucio. As much as it hurts you, you should get some rest as well."

"T-thanks."

"I appreciate your work, my friend. If something was to be needed from me, feel free to let me know. I'll be seeing you soon."

"Mhm, take it easy."

With that, we pressed on, heading towards where the Director was residing. A smile had crossed my companion. Despite trying to look professional, his emotions once more got the best of him. Knowing his friend had everything under control and the Okeanos were going to recover swiftly, I could not fault him feeling like that. It was then that I was once met with the lone mahogany door staring me right in the face. With a creek and push, we entered and were greeted by a man situated where I once met my companion. A lone rectangular plaque sat on the table beside him. It read:

Director Juri Aether

Chapter 17

3rd Moon

27th Phase

2018

6:48 pm

What dark room was when I first came here was met with a brilliant light, as the sun set on the horizon, orange and yellow tints covering the walls. Shadows were left cloaking his face, leaving a most ominous impressions. With his fingers crossed, the Director stared intently at me.

//Spooky!//

With a minute passed, the Director shifted his gaze towards my companion and finally shared his words:

"Case closed, I take it?"

"Of course."

"Any complications?"

"What were, have been resolved."

"As expected. Gushiken?"

"Troublesome."

He chuckled.

"Lucio."

"What?"

"When are you going to leave her alone?"

"As soon as she stops being stubborn and accepts our ways."

With a deep sigh, he shook his head in resignation.

"Honestly, you can be mature at times, but you can sometimes behave like a child."

"Tch."

Realizing who I was, he returned to me.

"You must be Jennifer Hawkins, yes? I'm sorry for not attending you anytime sooner. An emergency was brought upon me, so I had to leave everything to Lucio here."

"Oh, it is no problem, sir," I said. It is a pleasure to finally meet you, Director."

He smiled.

"Pleasures all mine. Allow me to formally welcome you, my name is Juri Aether and welcome to the Collective Detective Agency."

"A little late to be giving a grandiose welcoming, isn't it?"

"Ah"

Growing sheepish at his remark, he cleared his throat in embarrassment, to his amusement.

"In any case," he interjected, "It's so good to finally meet you, Ms. Hawkins. I knew that your father had a child, but I never imagined you would be the spitting image of him."

"You knew my Father?"

"But of course. We used to be partners back in the day."

"Really now!" I cried. "Father never mentioned you."

"Is that so? Well If he ever told you some of his adventures, then I'm sure it was to make it easy for you to understand. You were but a small child, after all."

"I guess so."

In pain, he squinted his eyes. Melancholy and bitterness haunted him.

"He was a bloody good inspector. Possibly the best of us all. And not only that, but, possibly my greatest friend. We all miss him dearly. My sympathies."

He smiled with a hint of sadness behind those words.

As the cold silence swam between us, my heart ached, for that, that I have lost. It feels like today was the yesterday that I once knew, but the yesterday that I once knew has been lost.

"He talked a lot about you. How you were a curious child and how you were always interested in our investigations. In fact," he paused. "You could say he knew you would choose to work as an investigator, for, he made me promise him to take you in as soon as you were ready to start working."

"I see," uttered my companion. "So that's why you wanted to recruit her."

"He did?"

"Yes. And I have been waiting for this day so that I may fulfill it. As soon as I saw your score and your name, I just had to make contact as soon as possible, so you could start working with us."

//Father planned this from the start then. How funny, even beyond the grave he is still looking out for me//

He smiled at my direction.

"But I would not wish to bring further memories that could bring you pain."

With a swivel on his chair, he collected some papers he had stored in one of the table drawers. Setting new directives he started to write with the beautiful quill he had on his left side.

"Going back to business, I take it everything went well, yes?"

"Y-yes! Thankfully, everything worked out thanks to Mr. Allegros directions and Ms. Okeanos assistance. I even helped solve a case on my first day!"

"You what?" he asked in utter shock. "Solve a case? W-what do you mean by solve a case?"

"Well, I was told that new recruits were shoved through a trial by fire to test their abilities. Is that not the case?"

"No, of course not! Why in blazers would we send recruits to solve cases? That doesn't even make any- wait a minute."

His shock shifted towards a suspicious glance towards Mr. Allegro. My companion, -looking away to not meet his eyes- felt the pressure of such gaze as a few sweat drops started to fall from his cheeks. Noticing, the Director squinted harshly, which my companion knew too soon.

"Lucio."

"Yeah?"

"Care to explain?"

//Hm?//

"Er."

"Did you take a new recruit to solve a case, again?"

//Again?//

"Heh, about that."

Shaking his hands in anger, he raised his voice, to many of our coworkers taking notice from the outside:

"Normal Tuesday right?"

"Lucio at it again. Why cannot the Director just fire him"

"What the devil is wrong with you!" He exclaimed in anger.

"If rookies can't even solve a case why have them here, Director!"

"Excuse me?!"

His soul piercing crimson eyes stared intently to Mr. Allegro. Flinching he grew aback by the pressure he tried to avoid.

"This would have never gotten through just by yourself. You might be a genius, but you're a fool when it comes to plans. Who else was in on this?"

"I may be malevolent, but I am no tattle tale."

"Lucio."

"Nope!"

Tensions flaring, I became a spectator at the back and forth tennis match between subordinate and superior.

"Hmph, well, see about that after I finish with you on practice."

"!!!"

At those words, my companion flinched even more, knowing what he was to expect of such a practice session."

//Good Lord! I never thought I would see the day he would feel fear!//

Looking towards me, I instinctively flinched. Realizing, He gave a deep sigh trying to control his temper.

"What nonsense," he glanced at Mr. Allegro. "I apologize on behalf of the Agency and this buffoon Ms. Hawkins. The trial by fire as you stated is nothing more than a farce. Only a fool would try to pull this off right under my nose. But don't worry, I'll be sure to sniff out the source of it all."

Trying to aleviate the conundrum, I try to soften the blow for everyone involved.

"I-It is no problem sir! On the bright side, we solved a case and saved an innocents person's life! And I learned by hands-on experience how to investigate! So it all worked out! Surely, there is no reason for anyone to be punished, is there?"

"Your kindness and heart is great, Ms. Hawkins. But disciplinary action is needed to keep people like Lucio in check, preventing them from not doing anything cheeky. The audacity. But I digress, if you said you're okay with how it all turned out then I won't do nothing for now. Now, I can see you as well have done your onboarding process, for I can see you have your Guardian with you."

"Yes sir! Thanks to Okeanos everything went smoothly as well! I still need to train with it but I know with everyone here I will be able to master it,"

"That's good to hear. Make sure you treat it right. If you can treat it well, it will treat you well in return. With a little training, I'm sure you'll learn to contr- hm? what's this?"

He extended his hand, and caressed my cheek, noticing the scar I had collected from our scuffle against the assassin.

"Where did you get these?"

"Get what?"

"The scars. They look like you've been positively cut."

"Oh! Umm"

Once again, he turned towards Mr. Allegro.

"Lucio."

Looking at him with his dead-pan eyes, my companion tried to avert his gaze. Trying to change the topic, he failed in a spectacular fashion.

"I apologize Ms. Hawkins but everyone's getting it tomorrow," he said with a smile across his face.I'm happy the case was solved, but next time be more careful Ms. Hawkins. Even if it includes disobeying your superior, do your upmost best to save your own life. You cannot save someone if you cannot even save yourself now, can you?"

"In the meantime," he looked at my companion. "Normally reports are filled by the lead investigator and assistant, but as additional punishment you will be in charge of filling the field report for both yours and hers."

"Ngh"

The Director gave a hearty sigh.

"But that is for later. Right now, we should show you where your office will be at."

"My office?"

"But of course! What kind of Director would I be if I didn't give you your own space? Come, come!"

As he stood up, I was given an image of the man who has been made in charge of this Agency. He was a wide-shouldered man, who wore an open-faced black kimono with a few bandages tied to his gut. Some sewed on pants tied with a green cloth was established around his waist. He was enveloped by a black and yellow jacket who stayed above his shoulders wherever he moved. He had two visible scars, each one on his cheeks. His hair -while similar to that of my companion- was tied down, silver and shiny, as pure as the heavens above and as clear as the bright sky.

We followed the Director to see where my office was. Mr. Allegro, per usual, was aloof and walking in his own disinterested way. After we reached the west side of the corridor, a lone door sat there.

"This is your new office," he muttered. "Would you care to do the honors?"

With a twist on the handle, the door clicked and opened. Finding the light switches, I quickly flick it and was greeted with the people I had met so far.

"Welcome to the Agency!, screamed everyone. At that, everyone pulled their own party poppers, leaving me in a bit of surprise."

"W-what is all this!"

"Heh," the Director smiled.

"Just a little something we had planned for your arrival!" cried, Ciarda.

"Planned?"

"Mm," my companion glanced. "Okeanos wanted to throw a little welcoming party for when you were done with your onboarding. At first, I was against the idea for I did not find the point of this party. But seeing how you were helping me close the case and how enthusiastic was Okeanos about the idea, I called ahead and told Ciarda and the rest to prepare this little presentation."

Taking everything in I was in disbelief at what had everyone had prepared for me. A table, some cabinets and even a telly with a sofa, in case I was to watch news and whatnot.

//Poor Ms. Okeanos. To think she had this planned out since the beginning, and now she is unconscious thanks my to impulses//

Thank you everyone! You have shown nothing but kindness to me! I just wished we had Ms. Okeanos here with us.

"Hm, well I think your wish is gonna be granted now more than never."

A voice suddenly echoed through the walls down the hall:

"Waiiiiiiiiiiiiiiiiiit!!!!!!"

Suddenly Ms. Okeanos came into view running as she had been wrapped with bandages across her head and arms. As she reached us, she stumbled for a bit, clasping her head at the pain she is still recovering from.

"Ngh, damn that smarts."

She pushed us from the side and stormed her way inside. Twirling towards Lucio she grew agitated.

"Damn it Lucio, I thought you weren't going to do anything!"

"I wasn't. However, I had a change of heart."

"No, you didn't! You just stole my idea!"

"That is probably the stupidest thing you have ever said all week, Okeanos. Why on earth would I do that? Besides, you barely just returned to us, and you still think you could have pulled this off on a limited time?"

"It doesn't matter!"

She rapidly starting Lucio in a comical manner.

"You decided to throw this party without me! The one who planned it! Me! What happened to waiting for me!"

"Well, we weren't gonna wait for you lass," Ciarda responded sheepishly. "We were told you were still recovering at the doc's."

"Besides," interjected Hypno, "what was worse, doing it without you or wasting all this that we had bought from our cold earned cash?"

"I didn't ask for your opinion, Hypno! Cork it!

"And you" she gazed towards the woman dressed in white. "Et tu, Snowy? "

The beautifully dressed and warm woman looked at Okeanos with her sky-blue eyes. She grew embarrassed, looking to her sides, not being able to confront her.

I'm sorry, I tried to convince them! I did! But they really didn't want to care for your feelings!"

"Convince us!" exclaimed Ciarda. What do you mean convince us? Last time I checked, you wanted to start eating all the food we had prepped up!"

"Ciarda please!"

"Figures" mumbled Okeanos.

Suddenly all the participants started arguing between each other. To his indignation, the Director grew frustrated, with his hands between his eyes.

//O-oh boy It would seem this party has turned from fun into discourse//

Behind us, Dr. Lewis walked casually towards us, scratching his head in embarrassment. To his notice, Mr. Allegro glanced at him in a contemplating way.

"You said you were going to keep her at bay, Lewis" said Mr. Allegro.

"Ha-ha, sorry Lucio. I tried, but as soon as she woke up, she asked about you guys and told her about the party. So, she just came running towards you guys."

"Wait," interjected Ms. Okeanos, "Where's Kag? And Qui?"

"Beats me. She's probably sleeping somewhere else and Quixote is probably in his lab tinkering. Blanc went and asked him to come, but he just waved her off like nothing, mentioning how this could decide the fate of the world, laughing in his typical nonsense."

"Confound it allllll!!!!"

"Trying to bring order again, the Director clears his throat loudly towards the attention of everyone.

"AHEM. This party is great and all. But I have a few questions for everyone. Can you explain to me why Ms. Hawkins was involved on the last case?"

At that, everyone grew big eyed.

"Ha-ha, w-what do you ever mean, Mr. Director?"

"Ciarda, spare me your usual nonsense. Everyone knows exactly what I mean. Well?"

"It wasn't my idea, I swear!" waved Ciarda in denial.

"Hypno?"

"I just thought it would be funny, heh."

The Director gave a very intently glare towards Hypno.

"But it wasn't my idea, Chief."

"So, no one did it then?"

I did, it was me, Director.

No, no, you didn't Blanc. Neither did Okeanos for she knew nothing of the sorts.

"W-what do you mean, sir?"

"Your injuries gave you away and your involvement."

"H-haha oh nooo I suddenly feel dizzy"

Hypno suddenly interjected.

"You ratted us out didn't you Lucio?"

"Why would I ever do that? I am no snake."

"He's right. He did not and for that reason everyone's getting some discipline for the next few days."

"What!"

"And no complaining or it's double for everyone."

//What is this an Agency or a parent running a family?//

"Honestly, I swear. Hm? Oh, sorry, Ms. Hawkins, this is just how it normally goes. You keep your eyes away for a few days, and this turns into a chicken coop."

After that, I gave a sudden burst of laughter, at all the events that have transpired. They grew curious and confused, for they did not understand the source of my humor.

"I apologize. I just think it is funny how everyone seems to be so close to one another. Ms. Okeanos I thank you from the bottom of my heart how kind you have been to me. I just wish I can repay that kindness some day as well to you, to everyone. I will not lie, I kinda feel out of place. And while the prank you people have concocted was an ill one at that, it did give me the push I needed to feel confidant in this career path. So please, Mr. Director, could you perhaps excuse them for this time?"

With that, he relaxed and gave a kind smile in return.

"Very well, considering you did help Allegro on this case, Ill grant your wish. You guys might have dodged a bullet there, but that won't happen again. If you dare to create mischief against Ms. Hawkins, you will surely get what's coming for you. Now! She's officially part of this Agency and for that matter she's part of this family. Treat her with the same respect you enjoy being treated. Now, now that everything is clear, I best believe it is time to enjoy between ourselves."

With those words, everyone let out a relieved sigh when suddenly a knock on the door came about. It was no other than Ms. Gushiken at the door.

"Ms. Gushiken!" I exclaimed. "What are you doing here?"

"I didn't want to be here, rookie. But, Okeanos told me how she was going to plan a party for your welcoming since yesterday. And seeing how I was involved on your first case, she called me to come. Here, I got you a little welcoming gift. I may not be an Agent like you but you did help us out, so thanks or whatever"

With that her cheeks became rosy, red, embarrassed at the sudden words she had uttered unexpectedly from her part.

//Ms. Gushiken//

T"hank you, Ms. Gushiken, for being so thoughtful and considerate. You know, you are not as bad as Mr. Allegro made you out to be."

"Oh, so that little rat has been talking behind my back now, has he?"

"With how much you like to talk who wouldn't."

"Why you little!"

Everyone started laughing together, enjoying this small piece of peace we were sharing together. After that, we began enjoying between ourselves as I got to know more each of the members that I was to start working together with for this year and hopefully for the next to come. I had the fortune of meeting Snow Blanc, the partner of Ms. Ciarda. She seemed reserved and quiet, but she seemed awfully sweet to everyone. She mentioned how she loves to cook and how she enjoys the cold weather. Her hair is of white color, blocking her right eye, as her hair is adorned with a snowflake designed barrette. She's older than me and Ms. Okeanos, but she roughly looks the same to us.

"Hey! Jenni, yoink!"

"H-hey! My camera!"

"Let's take a picture together! To commemorate Jenni's first successful case and first few days!"

"Nah, I'm good" said Hypno.

"Same here" replied Ms. Gushiken.

"That is so like both of you!" exclaimed Ms. Okeanos.

"I think that's a novel idea, Ms. Okeanos" interjected the Director.

"I second it, I think it is a wonderful idea. Here, I'll take the photo for everyone" said Dr. Lewis.

"I don't mind as well but" Ciarda gave a look towards Ms. Blanc.

"O-oh don't worry about me Ciarda. I'm not fond of photographs, but I do want to share a photo with Jennifer."

"So that's a yes then from everyone? Great!"

"Hold on, I didn't say yes."

Zip it! That's the least you can do for stealing my idea, buster!"

"Sigh"

"Great! Now you head over there, and you're over there. I think we're good, right? Great! Make sure to smile you three!"

"Heh. Now everyone group up. Everyone, say cheese!"

"Cheese!"

"Click!"

Chapter 18

3rd Moon

27th Phase

2018

5:44 pm

What dark room was when I first came here was met with a brilliant light, as the sun set on the horizon, orange and yellow tints covering the wallpaper. Shadows cloaked his face, giving an ominous impression on his display. With his fingers crossed, the Director stared at us.

//Spooky!//

With a minute passed, the Director shifted his gaze towards my companion and finally shared his words:

"I assume that you were working on the Victor Primo case. Case closed?"

"Naturally."

"Any complications?"

"What were, have already been solved."

"Brilliant."

"Oh, there was one problem. Gushiken was involved."

He chuckled.

"Lucio."

"What?"

"When are you going to leave her alone?"

"As soon as she stops being stubborn. It's only a matter of time until she opens her eyes."

With a deep sigh, he shook his head in resignation.

"Honestly, you can behave like a child sometimes."

Realizing who I was, he returned to me.

"You must be Jennifer Hawkins, yes? I'm sorry for not attending to you anytime sooner. An emergency was brought upon me, so I had to leave everything in Lucio's care."

"Oh, it is no problem, sir. I am just happy to meet you, Director."

He smiled.

"Pleasures all mine. Allow me to officially welcome you. My name is Juri Aether and welcome to the Collective Detective Agency."

"A little late to give such a grandiose welcoming, isn't it?"

"Ah."

Growing sheepish at his remark, he cleared his throat in embarrassment. On the other hand, I was enjoying the small introduction.

"In any case," he interjected, "It's so good to finally meet you, Ms. Hawkins. I knew that your father had a child, but I never imagined you would be the spitting image of him."

"You knew Father?"

"But of course. We used to be partners back in the day."

"Really now!" I cried. "Father never mentioned you."

"I don't blame him. When it came to work, your father was reserved when it came to sharing details. If he ever told you some of his adventures, then I'm sure he told them as simple as possible. You were but a small child, after all."

"I guess so."

In pain, he squinted his eyes. Melancholy and bitterness haunted him.

"He was a damn good detective, possibly the best of us all. And more than that, he was my greatest friend. My sympathies."

As the cold silence swam between us, my heart ached for what I had lost. It feels like today was the yesterday that I once knew, but the yesterday that I once knew had been lost.

"He talked a lot about you. How you were a curious child and how you were always interested in our investigations. In fact, he knew that this day would come, and made me promise him to take you in as soon as you were ready to start working."

"He did?"

"I see," uttered my companion. "So that's why you wanted to recruit her."

"Yes. And I have been waiting for this day so that I may fulfill it. As soon as I saw your score and your name, I just had to make contact as soon as possible."

//Father planned this from the start then. How funny, even beyond the grave he is still looking out for me.//

He smiled in my direction.

"But I would not wish to bring further memories that could bring you pain."

With a swivel in his chair, he collected some papers he had stored in one of the table drawers. Setting new directives, he started to write with the beautiful quill he had on his left side.

"Going back to business. Have you finally settled in with us?"

"Y-yes! Thankfully, everything worked out thanks to Mr. Allegro's directions and Okeanos's assistance. If it was not because of them, I would have helped solve a case on my first day!"

"You what?" he asked, dropping his pen. "Solve a case? W-what do you mean by solve a case?"

"Well, I was told that new recruits were shoved through a trial by fire to test their abilities. Is that not the case?"

"No, of course not! Why in blazers would we send recruits to solve cases? That doesn't even make any- wait a minute."

His shock shifted towards a suspicious glance towards Mr. Allegro. My companion, -looking away to not meet his eyes- felt the pressure of such a gaze as a few sweat drops started to fall from his cheeks. Noticing, the Director squinted harshly, which my companion knew too soon.

"Lucio."

"Yeah?"

"Care to explain?"

//Hm?//

"Er."

"Did you take a recruit to solve a case again?"

//Again?//

"Heh, about that."

Shaking his hands in anger, he raised his hand and slapped his head. Knowing that this was developing into something bigger, I slowly walk away. Raising his voice, our coworkers sighed outside, taking notice of what was happening."

"Sounds like a normal Tuesday."

"Lucio at it again. Why cannot the Director just fire him?"

"What the devil is wrong with you!" He exclaimed in anger.

"If rookies can't even solve a case, why have them here, Director?!"

"Excuse me?!"

With both their eyes staring at each other, they glared harshly. You could feel the aura coming from both men as they kept getting closer and closer.

"This would have never gotten through just by yourself. You might be a genius, but you're a fool when it comes to plans. Who else was in on this?"

"Hah, if you think you I'm going to talk, you got another thing coming."

"Lucio!"

"I'm no tattle tale!"

Tensions flaring, I became a spectator at the back-and-forth tennis match between subordinate and superior.

"Hmph, well, see about that after I finish with you in practice."

"?!!"

At those words, my companion flinched even more, knowing what he was to expect of such a practice session."

//Good Lord! I never thought I would see the day where I would see Mr. Lucio feel fear!//

Looking towards me, I instinctively flinched. Realizing, He gave a deep sigh, trying to control his temper.

"What nonsense," he glanced at Mr. Allegro. "I apologize on behalf of the Agency and this buffoon, Ms. Hawkins. The trial by fire, as you stated, is nothing more than a farce done by this idiot. Only a fool would try to pull this off right under my nose. But don't worry, I'll be sure to sniff out the source of it all."

Trying to calm down the situation, I try to soften the blow for everyone involved.

"I-It is no problem, sir! On the bright side, we solved a case and saved an innocents person's life! And I learned by hands-on experience how to investigate! So it all worked out! Surely, there is no reason for anyone to be punished, is there?"

"Your kindness and heart are great, Ms. Hawkins, but disciplinary action is needed to keep people like Lucio in check, preventing them from not doing anything cheeky. The audacity. But I digress. If you said you're okay with how it all turned out, then I won't do nothing for now. Now, I can see you as well have done your onboarding process, for I can see you have your Guardian with you."

"Yes sir! Thanks to Okeanos, everything went smoothly as well! I still need to train with it, but I know that with everyone here, I will be able to master it."

"That's good to hear. If you treat it right, it will treat you well in return. With a little training, I'm sure you'll learn to control it. Hm? What's this?"

Seeing the bruises and scars, he extended his hand and caressed my cheek, to which I wince a bit in pain.

"Where did you get these?"

"Get what?"

"The scars. They look like you've been positively cut."

"Oh! Umm..."

Once again, he turned towards Mr. Allegro.

"Lucio."

Looking at him with his dead-pan eyes, my companion tried to avert his gaze. Trying to change the topic, he failed in a spectacular fashion.

"I apologize, Ms. Hawkins, but everyone's getting it tomorrow," he said with disappointment in his tone.

"I'm happy the case was solved, but next time, be more careful, Ms. Hawkins. Even if it includes disobeying your superior, do your utmost best to save your own life. You cannot save someone if you cannot even save yourself now, can you?"

"I guess not."

"In the meantime," he looked at my companion. "Normally, reports are filled by the lead investigator and assistant, but as additional punishment, you will be in charge of filling both field reports. Complain and I'll give you something to complain about"

"Ngh."

//The Director really is tough. I would have to remind myself to not to make him angry.//

The Director gave a hearty sigh.

"But that is for later. Right now, we should show you where your office will be at."

"My office?"

"But of course! What kind of Director would I be if I didn't give you your own space? Come, come!"

As he stood up, I was given an image of the man who has been made in charge of this agency. He was a wide-shouldered man, who wore an open-faced black kimono with a few bandages tied to his gut. Some sewed on pants tied with a green cloth were established around his waist. He was enveloped by a black and yellow jacket who stayed above his shoulders wherever he moved. He had two visible scars, each one on his cheeks. His hair -while similar to that of my companion- was tied down, silver and shiny, as pure as the heavens above and as clear as the bright sky.

We followed the Director to see where my office was. Mr. Allegro, per usual, was aloof and walking in his own disinterested way. After we reached the west side of the corridor, a lone door sat there.

"This is your new office," he muttered. "Would you care to do the honors?"

With a twist on the handle, the door clicked and opened. Finding the light switches, I quickly flick it and was greeted by the people I had met so far.

"Surprise!"

"Bwuh?!"

"Welcome to the Agency!, screamed everyone. At that, everyone pulled their own party poppers, leaving me in a bit of surprise."

"W-what is all this?"

"Heh," the Director smiled.

"Just a little something we had planned for your arrival!" cried Ciarda.

"Planned?"

"Mm," my companion glanced. "Okeanos wanted to throw a little welcoming party for when you were done with your onboarding. At first, I was against the idea for I did not understand what the point of the party was. But seeing you helped me close the case and how enthusiastic was Okeanos about the idea, I called ahead and told Ciarda and the rest to finish the preparations before we got here."

"Would have liked it if you told us earlier. Just saying," complained Hypno.

Taking everything in, I was in disbelief at what had everyone had prepared for me. A table, some cabinets and even a telly with a sofa, in case I was to watch news and whatnot.

//Poor Ms. Okeanos. To think she had this planned out since the beginning, and now she is unconscious thanks to my impulses...//

"Thank you everyone! You have shown nothing but kindness to me! But..."

"But?"

"I just wished we had Ms. Okeanos here with us. I know she would have loved to be here as well."

"Hm, well, I think your wish is gonna be granted now more than never," remarked my companion.

A voice suddenly echoed through the walls down the hall:

"Waiiiiiiiiiiiiiiiiiit!!!!!!"

Suddenly Ms. Okeanos came into view, running as she had been wrapped with bandages across her head and arms. As she reached us, she stumbled for a bit, clasping her head at the pain she was still recovering from.

"Okeanos?!"

"Damn that smarts."

She pushed us from the side and stormed her way inside. Twirling towards Mr. Allegro, she yelled in anger.

"Damn it Lucio, I thought you weren't going to do anything!"

"I wasn't. However, I had a change of heart considering-"

"No, you didn't! You just stole my idea!"

"That is probably the stupidest thing you have ever said all week, Okeanos. Why on earth would I do that? Besides, you barely just returned to us, and you still think you could have pulled this off-"

"It doesn't matter! It was my party to begin with!"

Throwing a tantrum in a comical manner, we grew awkward about what was happening.

"You decided to throw this party without me! The one who planned it! Me! What happened to waiting for me?!"

"Well, we weren't gonna wait for you, lass," Ciarda responded sheepishly. "We were told you were still recovering at the doc's."

"Besides," interjected Hypno, "what was worse, doing it without you or wasting all this that we had bought from our cold earned cash?"

"I didn't ask for your opinion, Mr. deskceptionist! Cork it!"

//Deskceptionist?//

"And you," she gazed towards the woman dressed in white. "Et tu, Snowy? "

The winter clothes dressed woman looked at Okeanos with her sky-blue eyes. She grew embarrassed, looking to her sides, not being able to confront her.

"I'm sorry, I tried to convince them. I really did! But they really didn't want to consider your feelings!"

"Convince us!" exclaimed Ciarda. "What do you mean, convince us? Last time I checked, you wanted to start eating all the food we had prepped up!"

"Ciarda please!"

"Figures," mumbled Okeanos.

Suddenly, all the participants started arguing with each other. To his indignation, the Director grew frustrated, with his hands between his eyes.

//O-oh boy. This is not boding so well.//

Behind us, Dr. Lewis walked casually towards us, scratching his head in embarrassment. To his notice, Mr. Allegro glanced at him in a contemplating way.

"You said you were going to keep her at bay, Lewis," said Mr. Allegro.

"Ha-ha, sorry Lucio. I tried, but as soon as she woke up, the nurses told me that she had run off to the party. I tried to stop her, but I was not fast enough."

"Wait," interjected Ms. Okeanos, "Where's Kag? She said she was going to sing a song for us."

"She couldn't make it. She left an I.O.U note at the front desk."

"Ugh, nothing seems to be going my way today!"

Trying to bring order again, the Director clears his throat loudly towards the attention of everyone.

"AHEM. This party is great and all. But I have a few questions for everyone. Can you explain to me why Ms. Hawkins was involved in the last case?"

At that, everyone grew big eyed.

"Ha-ha, w-what do you ever mean, Mr. Director?"

"Ciarda, spare me your usual nonsense. Everyone knows exactly what I mean. Well?"

"It wasn't my idea, I swear!" waved Ciarda in denial.

"Hypno?"

"I just thought it would be funny, heh."

The Director gave a very intently glare towards Hypno.

"B-but it wasn't my idea, Chief."

"So, no one did it then?"

"I did, it was me, Director..."

"No, no, you didn't Blanc. Okeanos?"

"This is the first time I'm hearing about it!"

Hypno grew closer to Mr. Allegro and whispered to him.

"You ratted us out, didn't you Lucio?"

"Why would I ever do that? I am no snake."

"Then how did he find out?"

"He's right. He did not and for that reason, everyone's getting some discipline for the next few days. Each on their respective department."

"What!?" cried everyone in outrage.

"And no complaining or it's double for everyone."

//I guess he really is tough on everyone, regardless of department or years working.//

"Honestly, I swear. Hm? Oh, sorry, Ms. Hawkins, this is just how it normally goes. You keep your eyes away for a few days, and this turns building turns into a chicken coop."

After that, I gave a sudden burst of laughter at all the events that have transpired. They grew curious and confused, for they did not understand the source of my humor.

"I apologize. I just think it is funny how everyone seems to be so close to one another. Ms. Okeanos, I thank you from the bottom of my heart how kind you have been to me. I just wish I can repay that kindness some day as well to you, to everyone. I will not lie, I kinda feel out of place. And while the prank you people have concocted was an ill one at that, it did give me the push I needed to feel confidant in this career path. So please, Mr. Director, could you perhaps excuse them?"

With that, he relaxed and gave a kind smile in return.

"Very well, considering you did help Allegro on this case, Ill grant your wish. You guys might have dodged a bullet there, but that won't happen again. If you dare to create mischief against Ms. Hawkins, you will surely get what's coming for you. Now! She's officially part of this Agency and for that matter, she's part of this family. Treat her with the same respect you enjoy being treated. I have to go and finish some documents, but feel free to enjoy yourselves. Make sure to clean once everyone's done, though. Good night."

With those words, everyone let out a relieved sigh when suddenly a knock on the door came about. It was no other than Ms. Gushiken at the door.

"Ms. Gushiken!" I exclaimed. "What are you doing here?"

"Trust me, I'm not even sure. Okeanos told me how she was going to plan a party for you. And seeing how I was involved in your first case, she invited me to come. Here, I got you a little welcoming gift. I may not be an Agent like you, but you did help us out, so thanks."

With that, her cheeks became rosy red, embarrassed at the sudden words she had uttered unexpectedly from her part.

//Ms. Gushiken...//

"Thank you, Ms. Gushiken, for being so thoughtful and considerate. You know, you are not as bad as Mr. Allegro made you out to be."

"Oh, so that little rat has been talking behind my back now, has he?"

"With how much you like to talk, who wouldn't?" he said with humor behind his words.

"Why you little!"

Everyone started laughing together, enjoying this small time of peace we were sharing together. After that, we began enjoying between ourselves as I got to know more each of the members that I was to start working together with for this year and hopefully for the next to come. I had the fortune of meeting Snow Blanc, the partner of Ms. Ciarda.

She seemed reserved and quiet, but she seemed awfully sweet to everyone. She mentioned how she loves to cook and how she enjoys the cold weather. Her hair is of white color, blocking her right eye, as her hair is adorned with a snowflake designed barrette. She's older than me and Ms. Okeanos, but she roughly looks the same to us.

"Hey! Jenny, yoink!"

"H-hey! My camera!"

"Let's take a picture together! Us four who worked hard on Jenny's first case."

"I think that is a novel idea, Ms. Okeanos. Here, let me take the picture, Okeanos."

"Nah, I'm good. I'll pass," said Ms. Gushiken.

"C'mon Gushi please?"

With her crocodile tears, Ms. Gushiken does nothing but sigh, resigning completely.

"Okay, fine. But just one picture."

"Yay! Great! Then let's go!"

"Hold on, I didn't say yes."

"Zip it! That's the least you can do for stealing my idea!"

"Sigh. You can behave like a child sometimes."

//I am not sure you are in a position to say that.//

"Everyone group up. Now, everyone say cheese!"

"Cheese!"

"C-cheese."

Click!

Chapter 19

3rd Moon
27th Phase
2018
7:45 pm

As I continued to enjoy myself with the others, I noticed how Mr. Allegro was nowhere to be seen. I considered that he must have left a few minutes ago so I decide to check outside in case he might have gotten some fresh air.

//Heh, the least we need is himself getting into another fight.//

As I came to be on the lobby entrance, it was on south of the building that I was able to find him. He was standing on the curbside part of the bridge, gazing upon the celestial bodies. The brilliant moons illuminated the heavens as the stars danced around on the beautiful night sky. Suddenly, the Director came into view, and greeted me warmly.

"Ah, Ms. Hawkins. What are you doing here? I could've sworn you were inside with the others."

"Oh, Director. I plan to head back. I was just looking for Mr. Allegro. He sneaked away, so I was trying to bring him back."

"I see. Yes, he's wont to do that. He's not much of a partygoer as it is. Don't worry, I'll bring him back. Just enjoy yourselves with the other agents."

"Well okay. Please excuse me."

And with that, I continue where I had left off. Although my curiosity was piqued, I decided to follow orders and enjoy the rest of my night with my friends.

For the Director however, it was a different story. And it is with that I will expose the conversation that they had as soon as left them. Approaching the ace investigator, the Director chuckled in amusement, to Mr. Allegro's curiosity.

Well, you couldn't just stay enjoying the party now, could you?"

"You know how I'm not much of a partyer."

"And yet you were the one who stole Okeanos's idea?"

"Hm, was that supposed to be a joke?"

"Who's too say?"

"Heh."

"It wasn't the party, was it? You got something else on your mind."

His face growing furrowed, he contemplates to find the right words he wishes to express.

"Director."

"Heh, we aren't working right now, Lucio. You can drop the titles, son."

"Apologies. Dad, there's an issue I wish to bring with you regarding today's work.

"You just can't stop talking about work, can you? Well, what is it?"

"When I was speaking with Gushiken earlier, she told me how they were keeping a close eye on Facsimile, the criminal charged."

"Yes, that makes sense, and what about?"

"He was caught dead in his cell two hours ago."

Alarmed at this development, his display shifts completely, now more attentive than ever.

"Dead? How?"

"Gushiken mentioned that they're still investigating. But seeing there were no intruders or traces of anything, it's proving to be hard case to work on. However,"

"However?"

"I do recall that he was working with a certain figure. He mentioned a name, 'The Conductor'."

"Really now?"

"Yes. Considering he just gave away his name, I wouldn't be surprised if he killed him himself. And considering they have proven to be adequate in hiding among the public, he might have just infiltrated and just done the deed, like how that assassin did when she helped Facsimile escape."

Absorbed, the Director pondered at his words.

"That really is disturbing. But judging by those eyes, you still have more to share."

Pulling from his pockets, he retrieved the card he had collected earlier.

"I found this when Hawkins and I had our fight against the assassin. She left this behind. It's a cipher, but I'm not sure what it means. I was hoping that you could check it out, considering you have a talent for these sorts of puzzles."

Looking at it intently, he observes the nature of the card.

"Substitution," he said. "It should not be too hard to solve. Give me a minute.

With just a few minutes, Director Aether finished deciphering the code.

"Well? What does it say?" uttered my impatient companion.

With intrigue in the air, he shares the content of the card. It read:

The Conductor's assassin

The Rose Queen

For Consultation Call *** **** *****

Though he would never admit it, Lucio was impressed by how quick the Director had deciphered the message, something, not even a prodigy like himself could be able to do.

"The Conductor's assassin, huh? Well, we can at least surmise that your assassin really is connected to this Conductor fellow Facsimile spoke of. There's a phone number attached to the card, though I would expect the burner phone they used to be destroyed to kingdom come considering they're aware we are onto them."

Glancing, he reads Lucio's intentions.

"And I take it you wish for me to investigate it."

"If you could."

"When I get the chance with DoQuixote, I'll be sure to let you know. However, I'm not sure whether that's not the only reason you wish for me to look over, is there?"

Answering in silence, my companion gripped his hands in frustration.

"Dad," he said. "You know how we don't believe in coincidences, right?"

"Of course, nothing exists without a purpose. Everything has a reason."

Seriously, he stares at his father.

"I think the assassin we fought must have been Henley. And I'm not sure how, but it looked like she had a Guardian with her."

With the revelation in hand, the wind howled in suspense.

"Henley? Guardian? That's preposterous. She's dead, and the Guardian system became available for the agents after she died."

"I had my doubts first. But the more I looked at the way she moved and acted, the more I couldn't unsee her. Besides, it's not like we ever found the body right? I want to still believe that she's still somehow alive. If even a sliver of hope exists, I want to still cling to it."

Detecting the sorrow from his words, his father gives a pained expression. As if he too once passed through the same thing in the past. With that, the Director patted him on the shoulder, comforting him as much as he could.

"I know you do, and I don't blame you. And further I'll see what I can do. What concerns me is how she has access to the Guardian system. Both news are troubling for not only us but possibly the rest of the people. I'll look it over with DoQuixote tomorrow."

Grateful, he shares a nod.

"Does Gushiken know about this?"

"No, I haven't told her. Besides, it's not like she'd believe me. She would just think that I am growing delusional or doing some sort of twisted joke."

"But still, she's her sister. Even if you're wrong, I believe you should talk to her about it when you get the chance. Best to keep things as transparent as possible."

"I'll consider it."

"Brilliant. Now, try not to think of it any longer. I know you're not a fan of parties, but it might do you well to enjoy the fun," he said in a good humored tone. "Have a good night, Lucio. I'll see you-"

"Okay. Thanks."

"What's the real reason you brought the daughter of the Golden Sight?" he interjected. "There's more to it than simply fulfilling his dying wish, isn't there?"

With the unexpected question, the Director glances towards his son and simply replies:

"This country is bound to change. A wicked force from the shadows will soon engulf it with crime and darkness. We need all the help we can afford."

"Sir?"

" Besides, she's going to find the truth sooner or later. Best it being heard from the voice of our mouth. I'll let you know of any new information that comes up. In the meantime, have a good night son."

At those mysterious words, he withdrew from the night, leaving Mr. Allegro in thought.

"The truth?"

With that, he retraced his steps and returned towards the Agency, enjoying what remained of the night.

Epilogue

Some time after the report of Facsimile's death, a group of officers arrive at the scene of the crime. The body was found on the floor, and what came of it was nothing more than a corpse who suffered from bruises and broken bones. Discourse was happening, some suggesting that someone must have gotten inside, while others thought it could have been done by suicide. Amidst the chaos, however, a lone officer walked away from the crowd. Instead, adopting to leave the building and head straight to Green's trail, a scenic route that takes you to the countryside. With his hands tucked in his pockets, he greeted all passersby with positive energy, much to some of the stationed officers' curiosity. Within a few minutes of taking this route, he reached his destination, an abandoned church where moss and decay had overcome the man-made structures. Inside, a broken chandelier loomed inside, with rows of benches either broken or placed in file lines. Through a set of stairs that could be found in the back area, he descended until he found a secret chamber where a cast of shadowy figures were waiting for him inside, expecting him to arrive. With not a moment to lose, he directs his attention to the group.

"I assume everyone's here?" asked the disguised stranger.

"Yes, sir."

"Good. Was anybody followed?"

"No tail on my end, sir."

"Any tails were smashed to dust, hoo-ha!"

"..."

"I survived without a problem. Guess lady luck's on my side today."

"You opened us a window to get here. Considering they're chasing your ghost, that gave us plenty of time to escape."

"Terrific."

"I assume everything went well for you?"

"The officers are still as stupid as ever. And considering I killed him of using my Guardian, they're going to have plenty of time to consider the nature of the crime."

After getting a change of clothes, the party continued exchanging words.

"But still, who would have thought we had to kill Facsimile? He used to work here with us. Sure he got annoying sometimes, but to end this way?" said a young man.

"It is regrettable. Just like everyone here, he was raised here to work with us and contribute to a growing future. With the chemical knowledge he possessed, he could have done more than any of us could imagine. Unfortunately, his thirst for vengeance overcame his senses."

"Hoo-ha! But his family still wronged him though. Did we really have to kill him because he wanted justice?" said a gruff voice from the shadows.

"The sins of the past often haunt those that follow. As much as we try to run away from them, we can't. I'm sure the old headmaster there must have been suffering fatigue because of all the bad things his family had done, despite living as a saint. The weight of guilt is already enough, especially for someone who had nothing to do with that. Which would make sense why he even offered Facsimile a job to atone. And yet, in the end, despite our best wishes to turn his life around, he still stayed the same. Caving in his desire to kill the last line of the Cugini family, and, in the process, revealing our existence."

"So, what now? We target the people from the Agency?" said a lanky fellow sitting on a chair.

"And why would we do that?" replied a soft-spoken woman.

"Huh?"

"Outlaw, what is the code we are supposed to follow? The Conductor has told us specifically to only kill those that are swallowed by corruption or wickedness. Unlike the Bogshire Police Bureau, the Collective Detective Agency operates privately, and has made use of it by taking strides to maintain a clean independent identity. And as much as Web and I continue to investigate, nothing comes to light regarding any illegal or negative activities from their part."

"The Counselor is right. There's no point in meddling from our part. Besides, it's not even their fault now, is it Rose?

Reading the room, the group remains silence at the admonishment that was about to take place.

"S-sir I-"

"Who said you could help Facsimile perform this crime? Not only are you an accomplice, but your actions have stained our name in the underworld. And if it isn't bad enough, you also gave them our location thanks to your carelessness."

"Carelessness?"

"Where's your business card?"

Realizing that she must have left it at behind, she stood there, speechless, bowing her head in apology.

"I'm sorry. Facsimile mentioned that the headmaster was corrupt as well, so I believed him. And considering he wasn't one of us anymore, I just-"

"I have no need for your excuses. More than disobedience, I hate someone who has not set of values. That is why I kicked that snake out of our organization to begin with. And, for that matter, killed him in the process. The goes for anybody who does the same here. And that includes myself as well."

In silence, the hooded shadow stares on to the floor.

"In any case, we are to leave this place as soon as tonight. With our location compromised, we can't afford a minute to stay here. Outlaw, Pugilist, take all the burners and dispose of them immediately. Knowing the Director that oversees the Collective Detective Agency, he would most likely find a way to track us."

"Hoo-ha! Right away!"

"More work, huh? Well, not like I got anythin' else to do."

"As for the rest, pack all your necessities and head out. I'll contact everyone by our usual coms. You're all excused. Good luck."

With everyone receiving their orders, they all exit except for the hooded woman.

"I'll look away at what transpired today."

"Sir?"

"You were fooled and in your innocence, you believed in him. All because he used to be one of us, an old friend. But in this world, friends are hardly reliable. So, make use of this as a lesson. Don't expect me to do the same."

"Thank you."

With a glass in his hand, he pours some wine onto it all while playing some music in the room.

"You seemed distracted. There's something else. Isn't there?"

"Distracted? I'm not sure I-"

"Lucio was it?"

"How did you?"

"Come now, you know I have eyes everywhere. I take it he must have been your opponent."

"With nothing to say, she looks away.

"If you wish to return to him, you can. I wouldn't fault you if you wanted to go back to him. I still long for the warmth of my wife and the eyes of my child. But because I have unfinished business, I cannot yet go back. You're still young and I'm sure that even if you were to atone, you can-"

"I left the past behind, sir. And right now, all I want to do is get rid of everything that is polluting these streets."

"Even at the expense of being with him again?"

"Yes. Besides, he had his chance. It's too late for that now."

Satisfied with her conviction, he nods.

"Very well. Then make sure to not get anymore distracted. We've survived because of our silence, so we cannot afford another misstep."

"Right."

"Drinking his wine, his favorite score shows up on the gramophone."

"Ah, such a classic. Tell me, Rose, do you know what song this is?"

"I'm not sure."

"Sonata quasi una fantasia. Melancholic mood, is it not? It is a good score, for, as it plays out, the intensity grows higher and higher, contrasting the soft beginning. It was written by a musician who had a struggle with, well, I'll spare you the details, but let's just say he had struggled with outside forces. He wished to achieve his dream but was met with an unfortunate end."

"Like the premise, that is our dream. The group's vision: A change for the better. A change that will give future generations a sense of hope, even if it means fighting the darkness with darkness."

As he said those words, he crushed his wine glass with his hand, drops of wine dropping towards the floor.

"Some people wish to rip that dream from us."

"Clearly, they do not know who they made an enemy out of."

"Naivety at its finest, my dear Rose. But I welcome a good challenge. 'A dream without obstacles is no dream at all'. Quaint saying, but true, nonetheless.

Finishing those words, he lighted a matchstick, throwing it towards the curtains, a flame rising with great power.

"If they wish to involve themselves, then let them. We'll play with them for a while and see what is that they're really made of. Only then will they know who the Conductor and his Dark Sympohny is. Come, there's work to do."

www.ingramcontent.com/pod-product-compliance
Lightning Source LLC
Chambersburg PA
CBHW070630170726
48291CB00003B/954

* 9 7 8 1 9 3 3 1 2 1 3 8 3 *